The STORY Is the THING

Cover paintings and design, drawings and author photo by
Steve Atkinson, OPA.
Visit www.SteveAtkinsonDesign.com
and www.SteveAtkinsonStudio.com

Interior by Kelsey Rice

For Gail

Ain't that just like a human? Here comes that rainbow again.

—Kris Kristofferson

Joy was not made to be a crumb.

—Mary Oliver, *Don't Hesitate*

Don't you turn your back on your angels.
Don't run from the song of your soul.
Ride good horses. Raise strong children.
Pet your dog when he's growing old.
Let God's light shine down upon you.
Let the healing waters flow.
Don't you turn your back on your angels.
Don't run from the song of your soul.

—Mike Beck, *Your Angels*

The
STORY
Is the
THING

Amy Hale Auker

𝑷

Pen-L Publishing
Fayetteville, Arkansas
Pen-L.com

The scene could have been from an old Western filmed in black and white, from a time before cell phones or man-made satellites or hybrid cars or bombs dropped halfway around the world by engineers in Tucson, Arizona. Or margarine, something the old man on the bay horse despised. He bought salted cream butter like his mother churned when he was a boy, and he left it sitting out on the kitchen table in a ceramic butter dish that he washed when it got too greasy.

A sharp observer of the trio moving across the high Sonoran desert could have picked out hints of modern times like the rubber soles on the old man's boots, the machine-made shoes on the hooves of his livestock, and a jet airplane overhead making its run from L. A. to Phoenix.

A closer, more intimate examination would have revealed a MADE IN CHINA tag inside the collar of the man's shirt.

The old man on the stocky bay horse had been cowboying on this outfit, the Benson Ranch, for over fifty years, had arrived when the Benson and the 3R, the ranch to the south, had been all one holding. He had seen so many changes in his lifetime that he noted them less with surprise than with small ticks in his mind like the shorthand in his tally book. The lines on his face were from sun and wind and work and years. The pack mule in his hand, though old and rich in the wisdom of mules, was young compared to the man. The little dog that came behind them, sniffing and circling and ignoring his own painful joints, was even younger still.

The man's name was William Morgan, at least on his income tax return. Most people called him Uncle Bill, even though he wasn't anyone's real uncle. His pockets were always full of Juicy Fruit gum, butterscotch candies, and Brach's Toffee Royals. He never seemed to run out, though he patted the front of his shirt in mock horror when the ranch children came running up to him. Uncle Bill never left someone's house without a covered plate of leftovers or a grocery bag heavy with garden truck or half a cake wrapped in foil which he assured the women he ate for breakfast in case he didn't live until dinnertime. He was every little girl's favorite dance partner when the cowboys played music in the barn on a Saturday night, and he treated each one as if she were a grown-up lady, spoiling her for the rowdy boys with no manners who rough-housed out in the gravel yard. He made the real grown-up ladies wish they were little girls again.

The month was July. The trail was dusty. From its place in the midday sky, the sun burned hot on the little group. The day would get cooler from here on out. Bill didn't lift his eyes to the sky nor to the granite rock around him. He studied the ground, keeping the tracks he was following on his left most of the time, becoming more and more sure of his destination as they wound amongst the boulders, through the heavy brush, and past the occasional cactus that he had witnessed, in his lifetime, creeping slowly up into the piñon and juniper forest.

As the trail began to change, to tip off of the flatter mesa toward a lip where the world gave way, the horse's ears moved and pointed. The little dog's tail fanned back and forth, but he stayed behind at the mule's heels. Bill absently fingered the leather button on his chap pocket, the one where he kept the pistol.

"I knew it would be you." A girl stepped from behind a boulder and into the trail. She was blonde and sturdily built, not heavy, but solid and strong. Her face was shadowed by a black felt hat, and she was dressed in Wranglers and a denim work shirt of the same brand. They were men's clothes, but no one would mistake her for a man, not even with the beat up boots and the leather belt around her waist that kept her knife in its scabbard close to her hand. Bill didn't start at her sudden appearance in the trail. He reined up and looked off the lip of the canyon to his right before he stepped down.

"Told Julia I figured you'd show up." The girl moved forward on the trail and the old man jerked his head back at the sight of her face.

"That goddamned stinking son of a bitch." The words were simple and to the point, less of a knee-jerk cursing than an honest opinion.

"I'm okay. I'll be okay." Charlie touched the corner of her closed left eye and licked the split in her lip that kept popping back open.

Bill stepped up and touched her arm gently, ducking his head, better to see under the brim of her hat.

"Yeah." He let out a big sigh. "You shoulda come to me, girl. You shoulda come to me a long time ago."

Charlie looked at the ground, "I know."

"Well, you didn't, and I didn't see good enough what was going on." The old man grunted and then turned back to his animals. "I'm sorry for that. But we can't go back. We'd all best pick up our chins and look forward. All of us. Now, I assume you got a camp around here somewhere?"

3

He squinted at the girl over his shoulder, a grin on his face even though his eyes were wet, maybe just an old man's reaction to the sun shining brighter as it slid off its apex and down towards the west.

Katy Benson pulled her ski jacket up around her ears before she got out of the ranch truck with a Rocker B stenciled on both door panels. She stepped into icy wind that carried the smell of moisture from the southwest, drug her duffle bag and a hard-sided camera case out behind her. The little metal gate with a heavy spring clanged shut as she walked up the flagstone path and climbed the steps onto the wooden porch of the old house. The door was unlocked, testimony to how far the ranch camp lay off the pavement, tucked into a remote corner of the map. She dropped her bags inside the door, going back to the truck for a rolled-up sleeping bag and two bags of groceries.

"Spring, my ass," she muttered as she finally slammed the door with her shoulder. It was chilly indoors, too, but the water dripping steadily into the kitchen sink told her that the pipes were not frozen.

Katy put a match to the pile of newspaper and kindling laid neatly inside the open maw of the wood-burning stove. In the winter the squat stove was the focal point of the room that served for living, dining, and cooking. When the kindling burned brightly, she added a log and shut the door, setting the damper about halfway until the log caught fire. The air grew slowly warmer as Katy spread her sleeping bag on the couch so the down filling could lift before bedtime. She stowed away the groceries in the familiar kitchen before digging in a cabinet for an enamelware teapot and setting some water to boil on the gas cook stove, though she was looking forward to something stronger later on. The bottle she had bought now rested beside a half-drunk bottle of Wild Turkey 101 on the shelf above the stove.

Katy leaned against the sink and touched a hand-thrown pottery coffee mug upside down on the drain board beside one tin plate, one fork, a highball glass, and a ceramic butter dish, also upside down. The room was familiar to her, but the tall young woman felt like a stranger on this evening—as if she had wandered onto the set of a play after the actors had gone home and the stage hands had turned off the lights. The props rested lightly, waiting for the action to begin again.

The round kitchen table was cluttered with a deck of playing cards—worn soft by hundreds of hands of solitaire, an old-fashioned plug-in percolator, salt and pepper shakers that matched the candy dish that would have made an eBay collector drool. She knew without lifting the lid that it was filled with caramels and butterscotch candies. A crossword puzzle book cradled a pencil atop a much-worn Webster's dictionary. A pair of leather work gloves. A plug of chewing tobacco with one bite out of it. A tin ashtray full of livestock needles, various screws and nails, a lonely toothpick, and a piece of flint that might or might not have been an arrowhead. A spittoon rested beneath the edge of the table. On the seat of the chair closest to the door, a bare blonde crescent shone where the finish had been worn away.

Katy had no idea what the next few days would bring, but she was betting they'd be more peaceful than the last few. Two days before, she'd sat in a lawyer's office with no idea, really, why she was there. The day before that, she'd attended a funeral. Neither place had been exactly cheerful, and the funeral had been downright miserable with solemnity and pomp and hymns that had nothing to do with the old man who had been her friend. Sitting in the over-warm church in the unfamiliar pew, Katy had felt as if she had been shooting the rapids on a rushing river for several years only to round a bend and find herself becalmed. That same feeling swamped her now, standing in Uncle Bill's kitchen.

The flames under the teapot hissed and were answered by those in the stove where the oak log was catching up to the more readily burning cedar. A strand of wire ran from above the window by the sink to the opposite wall, a jerky line, a fact known only to those who had watched worn hands slice flank steak into thin strips and hang them to dry. Bookshelves lined one whole wall of the living area. To Katy's eyes, the loneliest spot in the room was the old recliner pulled up close to the stove. Beside it lay a stack of recent magazines, a novel sporting a bookmark from the local used book store, and an open fiddle case. The varnish on the fiddle glowed with a warmth that matched the fire.

Katy opened a cabinet and found a round mug, leaving the coffee cup Bill always drank from in the drain board. By the time she had a cup of hot tea in her hands, the room was warm enough for her to toss the ski jacket on the old recliner making it look less lonely and deserted. She reached into one back pocket of her jeans and pulled out a smartphone that she tossed on top of her duffle bag. The thing was useless way out here. From the other pocket she pulled out a folded envelope that held several sheets of yellow legal paper covered in handwriting. She'd read them many times since the lawyer had handed them over, but it seemed right somehow, to read them again, in the place where they had been composed. She

flattened the pages in front of her on the kitchen table and
took a sip of scalding tea.

January, 20—
Dear Katy,
I enjoyed your brief visit the other day. It did my old heart good to
see your long legs climb out of the ranch truck instead of Mark's. It's
nice, my dear, to have you back in the country—though I will miss
your postcards from places this old cowhand will only read about.
You won't get this letter for a long time to come, I hope. When you
do, the lady lawyer who gives it to you will also be giving instructions
to other people. She'll tell Hope to stay out of my things. She'll ask
Mark to make Cottonwood Camp nice for you, and to leave you
alone while you do as I am going to ask.

Katy looked again at the slowly dripping faucet and the split wood
stacked neatly on the hearth. Trust Mark to follow instructions.

Go to Cottonwood, Katy-girl. On the top shelf of the closet in the
bedroom you will find a pile of yellow tablets. Take them down and
read them for me right here, right here at my kitchen table or sitting
in my ratty old chair if you can stand it. I have no idea what you are
going to think when you get this bunch of rambling in an old man's
handwriting. My third grade teacher despaired of my penmanship,
and it hasn't improved much since. But, I hope that you will at least
understand the gist of what I started writing in the fall. Most of it
is self-explanatory, perhaps even the "why" of the writing. I didn't
have a reason, when I set out, other than to tell the story of this

past summer, the story of Charlie and Julia and Slide Canyon and their stay here at Cottonwood Camp. I wanted to tell my part in the whole sorry mess, but I'm not certain I got the job done.

Somehow, a whole lot of my life got mixed up in the story, and I just let it stay. Seemed like I must have needed to write it down. I hope I have left enough for you to understand what really happened. Truth is, I don't much care what you do with this story, only that you know it, that you hear it, that one person on the planet carry the truth lightly, gracefully, through a few more years.

You are smart, Katy. Savvy in an old person's way sometimes. You have a legacy to manage in this ranch someday, plus a hard old world to do it in, seems to me. I've told you this before, but bear with me for I need to put it down in writing. Your uncle was the best friend a man could have ever had. I not only admired him, looked up to him, learned a lot from him, but I loved him. We shared a lot of our lives, a lot of long hard days, a lot of drinks, a lot of decisions. You are like a gift to me from him, given after he died. Over the last several years, I have enjoyed getting to know you via letter and postcard, but also in the few times you've come out and stayed here at the camp. I think, for the most part, you and I are the only ones who really know about those getaways, as you called them.

Do you remember the first one? I sure do. Never before has a beautiful young woman come a'callin' at my house with a bottle of Jim Beam and such pure intent. If I recall, you set out to do three things: listen to me fiddle, see the legendary sunset over Cottonwood Canyon, and get drunk. We accomplished three out of three, didn't we? I covered you with one of Hope's old quilts on the couch long

9

after the sunset was over, long after the music had stopped, long after the glasses were empty. I don't remember what demons you were drowning that time, but I remember the ones you came to drown later on . . . when your mother died, when you graduated with no idea what you wanted to do with your degree, and once, drowning the mean words of a hairy-legged boy. Then you left me, Katy-girl, left me to go wander the world. I thought of you often, and wondered who was going to cover you up when you were on the other side of the globe, taking wonderful photographs.

Thank you for those getaways, for those photographs, for what I am certain you are about to do for me now that I am gone.

So, down to business. Besides all of the words I have written down, I am also leaving you with some tasks. I've made arrangements for my ashes to be given to you.

"Shit!" Katy jumped up from the kitchen table. She jerked the door open, ran out to the truck—ducking her head against the increasingly bitter wind—and came back in, breathless. She placed a dull pewter urn on the top of the bookshelves, standing on tiptoe to get it up where it blended into the shadow of the ceiling, and then went back to the table, warming her hands again on the mug.

I've made arrangements for my ashes to be given to you. Take them to Cottonwood Camp, and store them somewhere. There is a little book of poetry, handwritten, beside my bed. The book can go back to Anna now. Inside the cover is a phone number. It is your job to call and tell her I am gone. She will know what to do with my ashes.

Attached to this letter is a list of my belongings with instructions about who to give it all to. It is only stuff—no precious treasures—just silly pieces of an old man's life—but it is a comfort to me to imagine giving it to those I love. There is an olla, on the bottom shelf of the big bookshelves, one that was glued back together from fragments of pottery. That is for you, Katy. I know you will take care with it, appreciate the ancient hands that made it from the clay of this land. Perhaps even appreciate the hands that put its pieces back together.

Every book on the shelves has a slip of paper in the front with a name on it. I can't bear to pack them up myself any time soon. They are my friends, in every sense of the word. I've mainly kept the ones that grabbed me and changed me and never let me go, just like some of the people who wander into our lives. I've donated many to the little sale those ladies down at the library have, let them go on their way out of my life and into someone else's.

Anna's wooden trunk is at the foot of my bed. Please make sure she gets it when she comes to scatter my ashes. The coffee mug I always drink out of belonged to her from the beginning. Put it in the box if you will. My fiddle goes to her as well. Everything else is on the list.

I am glad you've come home. And now you've been saddled with this story, with a whole pile of pages. If you are reading this, I hope they will soon be safe in your hands. Do the right thing by them, Katy-girl. You are the right person for the job.

If you get a chance, go hug on Charlie. Speak kindly to Julia. Help Mark carry his secrets forward without suffering. Listen to Anna . . . she has become a wise woman.

And Katy, welcome home.
All my love, Uncle Bill

Katy laid the letter aside and went through the rapidly dimming room to the closed door of the only bedroom. She hugged her arms around herself in the cold air, and then reached for the taped-together and falling-apart book on the bedside table. She opened it to see fragile, worn pages covered in faded ink written by a hand that seemed young and strong. Inside the front cover was the name *Anna* followed by a phone number. This part was written in recent ink in handwriting that had become familiar to her from letters in airmail envelopes and even more familiar in the past two days from the oft-folded pages in her back pocket. After retrieving the stack of yellow legal pads from the top shelf of the closet, she backed out of the cold room, turning out the light, and shutting the door. She laid the stack on the table, added some steaming water to her tea cup, and set the still-hot kettle on the woodstove rather than the cook stove.

The pages in front of her gave Katy a feeling of reverence, of new beginnings, incongruous perhaps with the idea of death she'd been faced with for the last several days. She liked the rightness of being settled into Uncle Bill's home as she switched on the lamp and began to read. The sky grew lavender and then gray through the window. The wind carried a flurry of dry flakes down to dance among the newly greening cottonwood trees in the creek, but Katy never noticed.

Old men don't sleep much. Maybe we slept too much as young men, or maybe, deep down, we know the big sleep is coming.

Whatever the reason, my brain and my bones won't let me sleep much nowadays. Neither will this story. It is the first thing on my mind when I wake in the early morning hours and the last thing on my mind when I shut my eyes at night. I can't tell, now, the difference between the real thing and the story my mind has played like a movie, over and over, even the scenes I had to make up because I wasn't there. And, the parts that are the most real, the parts where I was there, well, they stay with me like a stain, and maybe writing them down will be the best way to lift them off my mind.

They say that there are no new stories under the sun, and while that may be true, I read an interview with a famous writer once and he said something I will never forget. He said, "The story is the thing." Any time a new song comes out of the radio, or I read a new book or a new poem, or even see a painting or a photograph, that line comes to me. Once I went to a dance recital to watch a bunch of the little girls from the ranch. As those children bumbled their way through a ballet piece and another more upbeat tune, I thought that it probably applies to almost anything. It applies to the tracks in the dirt that tell me where a mama lion is bringing her cubs to drink or whether the cows are coming down the slope or going back up or where the elk are jumping the fence or if a bear is the reason there are no cows in the canyon in early spring. Even the water in the rain gauge and the smells on the wind are telling a story. The story is the thing.

And this is quite a story. Sure did stir things up around here. Most people don't know much about my part in it. And perhaps they'd forgive me if they did. That's one of the great things about being an old man.

I don't think there has been much forgiveness for those girls, though. They didn't follow the rules, and as modern as the world seems to me, there are certain walls in the human mind that are hard to breach.

We'd all be much better off if we practiced tolerance rather than getting so dang good at judging. I don't judge harshly much anymore. I would say that I have seen too much, but that really isn't the case. I haven't seen much except a lot of sunrises, a lot of autumns, a lot of baby calves, a lot of new pavement stretching between the isolated and the populated. I've seen the way that a human being can't breathe in and out without making ripples in this big old pond. Perhaps the curse of growing old in decent health is that I am able to look back with clear vision on my life. I am helpless to do much about my mistakes, hasty words, or wrong turns, which makes the clarity painful.

One reason I don't judge others in their relationships is because I've been married twice and had my heart broke once. As an old man, I can honestly say that when the end of my life comes, I hope my heart is all used up, given away, worn out, and tired from all of the loving I've done. That's what a heart is for, after all.

When I decided to write in the hours before dawn when my bones won't let me stay among the sheets, I bought this six-pack of yellow legal tablets thinking I'd give the other five to the kiddos at headquarters who are always filling the backs of scrap paper with crayon and markers. But maybe I won't be so quick to give the extras away. Seems like this is a big story, and I wake with my head and heart so full of words that I don't even roll over and try to go back to sleep in spite of my aching hip.

I hit that hip on a boulder when Homer fell with me that time. My second wife said that in a normal person the hip-bone would have broken, but not me. Instead, the skin and muscles bloomed with all colors of the rainbow, and I had to take anti-blood-clot medication for the hematoma. But, broke or not, that hip complains constantly, kinda like that second wife. I'd like to say that she is the reason I am still here where I landed after Sally, my first wife, died, but the truth is I stayed because I fell in love with this country and I loved Richard Benson.

I came to this ranch when it was all one piece, the 3R, the Red River Ranch. Benson was in his prime. I came at a time in my life when I needed to be alone, needed to grieve and mourn. Benson gave me South Camp, and for those first few months, he pretty much left me to do those things. But one evening, uninvited, he showed up with a bottle and stayed the night. I would say that it was typical of Benson, but I don't know if it was typical of him in general or just typical of our friendship. Though he was the owner and the boss, he also became my friend starting that night as well as over coffee and eggs the next morning, and the friendship continued for many years. That friendship, more than any woman or paycheck, is what kept me here. I was loyal to his leadership, sure, but there was something more, something that bridged the spread between our ages and our positions on the ranch and in life.

This was back in the day when you had to love being alone for days on end to cowboy. Back when the reality was that if your horse fell and smashed your leg, you were on your own. Back when men rode for the brand. And I rode for Benson's brand. Still do, for that matter.

Benson was proud of the 3R brand, and it broke his heart when he had to sell that brand along with the southern half. Truth is the southern end always has been the better country, year in and year out. I didn't mind the loss of the brand since I always liked the Rocker B. It was our horse brand back then.

Damn that old man and his benevolent old ghost. I still can hear his voice in my head. One time in the late 70s when we had a warm wet winter, it started on to rain and snow for the whole month of March, right when we needed to be making a move from that upper Jones area off down into some of that lower bench country so I could get the cows all wadded up around the tanks with as many bulls as we could find so they'd get bred back when the calves really started coming. Every time I tried to put the crew together and get started, it rained or snowed or both. Finally, the ground dried out enough that we wouldn't cripple every horse on the outfit, and all the guys gathered at Jones Camp. I even hauled the cook and his groceries in there and called breakfast for six sharp the next morning. About three a.m. I woke up to hear rain on the tin roof of that old camp house, and it never did let up. I was pretty tightly wound back then, and I gave up on sleep around four, crawled out of my bedroll, and went into the kitchen. There was Benson, coffee cup already in hand, looking out a black window streaming with silver drops. "You know, Bill, I'll take a rain or a calf any day!" He raised his coffee cup to me in a cheerful salute and turned back to the window.

Richard Benson is the one who taught me the "cowman" side of this business rather than just the cowboy part. He knew cows,

THE STORY *Is the* THING

understood the markets, was savvy about when to hold and when to sell, when to jump on a fad and when to stick with more proven practices. Most of the hands didn't give him much credit. After all, he wasn't one of them. He was the owner, and that created, for many of them, a chasm they had no way of crossing, which is too bad, for to know Richard Benson was to know a fine man, a smart man.

There are many types of men who are drawn to cowboying, and I've met and worked with all of them. For some, it's the sport, the little bit of wild, the image, the romance, the idea. For others, it is all they've ever known, and they just aren't the type to strike out and see if they like pounding nails or reading law any better. For some, it's their love of the horse and the opportunity to spend a lot of time in the company of one.

There is another kind of man for whom cowboying means an opportunity to dominate, to pit himself against something and stomp it when it lies down whether it is a cow, a horse, or the terrain. I've never understood this attitude, and as time goes on, it gets harder and harder for me to stomach or even contemplate. I've come to believe that "do unto others" should apply in spite of species designation.

This life has given me a lot of time to think, to read, to study animals and men, especially during my stint at being the boss. I make noises about how a cowboy used to ride for the brand, but one of the things I figured out through all of my reading and watching is that men are men are men everywhere, whether on the high seas in a big ship or below ground in a coal mine, behind a string of sled dogs, on the moors of Scotland, or in every bar in every land. The same men *show up. There's always one who would rather climb a tree and lie than stand flat-footed and tell the truth. Always one who is trying to brand someone else's longears. Always one with a poem hid way down deep inside. Always one whose father beat the shit out of him as a lad. Always one who is having an affair with his neighbor's wife who is no prettier or sweeter than his own—just different. Always one who is like a plow horse plodding along, looking neither left nor right. Always one who starts drinking early in the day from a bottle hid high up on a shelf behind the horse medicine in the barn. Always one who is a born leader, and always one who thinks he is. Always one whose feet smell bad. Always one who can't read and always one who lives in the past, badmouthing the present. Always one who is so talented that he can't stand himself. Always one who beats his wife.*

We've got one of those around here. Or we did have.

Katy opened the heavy iron door, added a fresh log to the stove, and stood, arms crossed, smiling to herself while it caught fire. She walked over and lifted down the half-empty bottle of bourbon, poured a generous helping in the highball glass from the drain board, and added a few cubes of ice from the freezer. Standing in the middle of the room, Katy raised the glass, not to the urn on the shelf, but to the yellow pages on the table.

"Uncle Bill."

Julia often found that the map of life in her imagination was completely incompatible with how things were in reality, and this had been a problem since she could remember. Her parents bought tickets to the Nutcracker when she was a small child and prepared her by telling her the story of a Christmas party with toys that came to life. It took root in her mind, becoming something so vivid, so hers, that she fell asleep during the performance of the real thing. When she was older, she imagined kissing a boy. But when the boy was real, she felt let down by the urge to wipe his spit from her lips. When she went off to college, she had a fantasy of unfettered thinking and new doors opening. Instead she found an extension of high school that made her nonchalant about her studies.

Now she sat on the front porch of the general manager's house, smack in the middle of a real landscape. When she and Mark were first dating, she had drawn a vivid, yet simple map of the Benson Ranch in her head one night after a romantic dinner while they drank coffee and talked. Mark had explained that if the Benson Ranch were ironed out flat it might be 300 square miles, but on a topographical map it was just under half of that. He had talked of the canyons and mountains as a marriage of the piñon and juniper forest and the upper Sonoran desert. In her infatuated state it had sounded like poetry. She loved hearing him speak of the horses by name and about the people who were, at least in her imagination, both wholesome and earthy. Now she had to admit that the poetry was in her own mind and very little of it came from Mark.

Before she moved out here, she knew all of the details—or imagined she did. She knew that the ranch employed three cowboys living on camps spread out over the country. Usually had two single men living in the bunkhouse at headquarters, a cow boss, a mechanic, and a cook. She knew, without understanding, that it was a 45 minute drive from headquarters to the nearest small town, barely big enough to merit a zip code. She knew that whenever someone asked what kind of cows the Benson Ranch ran, Mark would grin big and say, "What kind do you like?"

In her head, Julia had painted a big fancy entrance leading from the highway and into headquarters, a lane lined with towering oak trees that would be especially appealing in autumn. On the true map, the one in which she found herself, none of the physical plant was visible from any paved road. To get to the highway, one had to get out of the pickup twice to open gates, getting out two more times to shut them behind. To the uninitiated eye headquarters was a jumbled heap of buildings, some of them quite shabby, the cook house indistinguishable from the bunkhouse, not to be confused with the barn with its long loading dock across the front. The "Big House" where the board of directors and the Benson heirs sometimes stayed was hidden behind old trees that had been there longer than some of the other buildings. The cow boss's frame house was distinguishable from the mechanic's house only by the jumble of children's toys in the front yard of the latter and the bright flowerbeds in front of the former. The general manager's house was the first one a guest encountered as he drove across the cattle guard into headquarters. There was no tree-lined lane.

Mark was young to be general manager, but he had been handpicked for the job by the man who last retired from the position. His selection was a matter of his father having run a large ranch all the time Mark was growing up, a matter of his having gone to college after spending a couple of years rodeoing and working on other ranches. It was, she realized now, a matter of knowing the right people and being willing to do an internship between semesters instead of playing at riding saddle broncs. It was a matter of Mark truly caring about both the bottom line and the blend of people, animals, and land under his leadership. It was a matter of his having chosen to take as many accounting classes as animal husbandry courses.

One of the most stressful times in Mark's year was his annual trip to Chicago to present the next year's budget and answer to the board for the year past. Even that had sounded romantic when they first met, and she had imagined herself accompanying him on the trip instead of staying behind.

One of the biggest challenges Mark faced was the enormous suck called payroll. He constantly questioned whether the ranch needed the mechanic who also did duty as the handyman, landscaper, and windmill man. Mark said that he'd never do away with the cook or the cow boss, but that sometimes when he looked out the window of his office and saw the mechanic smoking a cigarette beside the shop, he could smell sweet dollars slipping from the budget. Julia wondered if part of that was because Mark missed smoking his own occasional cigarette, now that he never indulged in anything remotely sinful.

Julia's map of the ranch had been replaced by real geography, and on the first warm evening of early spring, she sat on the front porch wondering what had happened to the fantasy map of her life. A pile of books and magazines rested in her lap, an empty wine glass on the wooden table at her side. The real map found her a married woman, married to someone with a lot of responsibility and not a lot of time or imagination for fun. The real map showed a derailed thesis leftover from graduate school, a wrinkle in the vows she had made, and a sense of inertia that, tonight, made her sit out on the porch long after adequate reading light had faded from the sky. The real map, she realized, was boring as hell. The real map required more red wine than was probably smart, but she kidded herself that it was good for the heart.

The western sky had been brilliant only moments before, but now it presented a graying face while the east was darkening to navy blue. When the breeze began to blow cold, Julia picked up her bookmark where it had fallen to the boards of the porch and shoved a yellow cat off her feet.

The slam of the screen door made Mark look up from his commentary on the book of Revelation.

"Go ahead and shut the big door, won't you? It's getting chilly in here." Julia shut the heavy door with her foot since her hands were full and barely made it to the bar that separated the living room from the kitchen before dumping her notebook, pens, highlighters, and stack of books. A magazine flopped to the floor at her feet when she opened her arms to let the pile tumble onto the countertop. She set the wine glass down with a clink.

"The sunset was gorgeous," she threw over her shoulder as she stepped over the magazine and went around the end of the bar. She ate a bit of leftover steak from a plate by the stove, salted a leftover slice of potato and ate that, too. She considered the boxed red wine she had resorted to now that Mark didn't drink his share when she opened a bottle of merlot.

"Huh?" Her husband looked up again from the thick book in his lap.

"The sky. It was every shade you can imagine for just a moment."

"Oh! Good! Ready for bed?" He stood and stretched while Julia put her glass in the sink, deciding against a refill. Mark stooped down to pick up the magazine and placed it on the helter-skelter pile on the bar. "Do you need any of this?" He gestured at her mess as she walked by, headed down the hallway.

"Na . . . I'm fine. Hey, did you get a chance to put that dinner invitation in Charlie's mailbox when you went to the 3R?" Julia stopped in the door of the bathroom and looked back at him. Mark shook his head. "Yeah. Well, I mean, I handed it to Charlie. She was there. Didn't need to put it in their box."

"Oh! Cool! Did she say anything?"

"Just thanks." Mark put toothpaste on his toothbrush and reached to turn on the shower. It drove Julia crazy that he let the water run down the drain while he brushed his teeth and took off his clothes.

"I'm glad we are going to get a chance to witness to that young couple, but I am not sure that the idea of them actually eating dinner over here is all that great," Mark mumbled around his mouth full of foam. "I mean, it'd be nice for you to have a friend and all, but there are lots of young women in the church you'd like." He spit in the sink. "Who might be a better choice than Charlie."

Julia scrubbed at her own teeth, trying to ignore how much hot water was running down the drain while Mark hung his Wranglers on a hook on the back of the door and dropped his socks, T-shirt, and work shirt in the hamper after emptying his pockets into a wooden tray beside the sink.

"I like her is all. I just thought she would be someone different to hang out with." Mark stepped into the shower and grunted, she wasn't sure if in appreciation for the hot water on his skin or in acquiescence to her. She grabbed a worn college T-shirt off the floor where she had dropped it that morning and threw her clothes toward the closed hamper knowing that Mark would put them in neatly before he came to bed. The very knowledge made her back teeth itch.

"It's a bad idea, Julia!" Mark hollered over the sound of the water as his wife left the bathroom, thumping the door closed behind her.

When Mark came into the bedroom, Julia looked up from where she sat cross-legged in her little pool of lamplight, a book propped open on the covers in front of her as she rubbed lotion into her hands. She was struck by his huge handsomeness, his simple dearness. He was damp-headed and wearing sleep pants with pine trees on them. She felt his fatigue as if it were tangible, coloring the air around him. She reached to pull back the covers on his side of the bed, patted the cool sheets in invitation, wishing she hadn't thrown her clothes on the floor. He sighed and seemed about to sit down on the edge of the bed, but changed his mind.

"Just a sec." Mark went into the living room to retrieve the commentary before crawling in beside Julia, turning on the lamp on his side of the bed. Within minutes, he was snoring, the heavy book open on his chest. Julia put her own book aside, picked up the commentary, and glanced at the bold title words on the page.

"Marriage supper of the Lamb," she read aloud quietly. She dropped the book to the floor with a thud, leaned across her sleeping husband and switched off his lamp. Julia lay in the dark for several minutes, flat on her back, staring at the narrow band of moonlight at the top of the curtains, before she whispered, "But I don't want to witness to them."

Charlie's story as told to Katy Benson, Cottonwood Camp

Lots of people thought I left Cody Jack because he hit me. But that's not true. I told that sorry mess of bones I was leaving him exactly three weeks before my first black eye and bloody lip, and several months before all of the bad stuff happened. And I meant it, too. I meant what I said—that I was leaving him.

I'd had black eyes before, just never from a fist. Mainly from my own clumsiness or trusting a horse too much. My cousin's kid gave me a black eye once when I leaned down to kiss his sweet little head—and he jumped up high like kids do—at just the wrong time. Come to think of it, I got a fat lip from that deal, too.

Cody Jack pushed me around some before that, mainly when he was drunk, but that's not why I told him I was leaving. I mainly decided to leave Cody Jack because things died or got maimed and crippled around him all the time. I didn't want to be next. I didn't want to die or end up with a limp. We already had a three-legged dog, a cat with no tail, and a cat with a broken back that walked all side-wise. Cody Jack had crippled two ranch horses and one horse he was riding for a lady in town. One of our personal horses was so dinked out that no one could make a whole day on him. He had also wrecked his truck, broken both screen doors off their hinges, and rid our kitchen of every breakable dish. I just didn't want to be the next broken thing.

When I met Julia, she agreed with me, wanted me to leave right then, and maybe I should have left sooner—and maybe I would have been better off, but who knows? I'd have missed out, too. Missed out on knowing what I could really do, missed out on knowing Julia. Who knew she'd end up hurt right along with me?

I told Cody Jack I was leaving him at the beginning of December, but he just laughed at me.

"You can't leave me, Charlie. You have too many animals. No way is your mama gonna let you take four horses, two dogs, and however many cats to her house. You got no job, no money, and no way to haul all them critters. No, baby, you'd better stay with me if you know what's good for you."

I guess he thought he'd told me. And a few weeks later he came home all hopped up on somethin'—or maybe he was just drunk—I never could tell—and I guess he showed me. But a man's fist never showed a woman nothin' is what Julia says—'cept how stupid the man is—how fragile his ego is and how small his dick is. I don't know about fragile egos—and Cody Jack's dick never seemed small to me when I was paying the price to feed all of my animals and live at Live Oak Camp.

At Christmas Cody Jack gave me another horse. He made a big romantic deal out of driving over to headquarters to get my gift and driving back into the yard all starry-eyed—as if the pretty little roan mare would make up for everything. My cheekbone was yellow from a healing up bruise, and even I could count that five horses was more than the four I already had. Funny how a man thinks. Here Cody Jack was—not even owning his own truck—driving the ranch truck everywhere even when he wasn't supposed to—and when he finds enough dough to actually buy himself some wheels—he goes off and gets us another mouth to feed. When I told Julia that part of the story, she got tears in her eyes, and she looked so sad. But we all looked pretty sad later on, in the summertime.

I met Julia at headquarters, 3R headquarters. She came over with another gal to drop off a petition or something to bring better internet and phone towers out this way. I was loading horse feed to take back to Live Oak. I guess it doesn't matter what all was going on that day—'cause really it was just a day. Julia walked over and introduced herself and then started putting sacks of feed on the tailgate while I stacked them. I was glad that it was one of those times when I didn't have any marks on my face because she was so pretty. And I thought she was dainty—as in, not tough. She is like a messy fairy, something from another world, all pale skin and wild hair. But I found out later that Julia is anything but dainty—and plenty tough.

I wish Julia could tell this story. I hope you ask her to tell you her part, Katy, because she'll do it so much better. She'll get all of the facts straight. That day I first met her, I remember thinking that she was the daughter my mama wished for. I imagined that her house would be all clean with things hanging on the walls, something other than plastic, tin, and cast iron in her kitchen, no dirty clothes piled in the shower, the beds made, no fist-sized holes in the walls, and I'd have bet all her house plants were alive, too. All of mine had died a few months before, except the aloe vera, when I was off taking care of my Pa Paw when he got sick in New Mexico. The aloe vera just got maimed, its arms smashed or broken off where one of Cody Jack's friends fell on it, acting like a fool in the living room. Of course, replacing them is easy for me. I root cuttings from everyone's plants around, sometimes even digging up plants from the pasture to see how they'll do indoors.

Julia was all clean, dressed like a girl, shiny. She isn't very big, you know, and I noticed her tiny hands and red hair, how her skin is all smooth and white. Sometimes she wears strange things that no one else would think to wear, like a scarf around her ankle or men's cologne or a hat with a red rose on it with a pair of cutoff jeans. She isn't trying to be weird or show-offy. She's just like that. She's quirky and, well, you know, sometimes *clueless*.

She thinks the whole world is good, even after going to college. She'd rather read a book than watch a movie, not like most people—well except Uncle Bill. She listens, really listens, when people talk. She can say poetry, even the kind that doesn't rhyme, just like Uncle Bill used to. They even knew a lot of the same poems.

I met Mark about a week later. He gave me a note, not a folded up piece of notebook paper like high school kids pass back and forth, but a real note card, tucked inside a matching envelope with my name on the front. Most people wonder about my name. My folks named me Charlotte, but by the time I was a week old, everyone was calling me Charlie. My sister's name is Antonia and everyone calls her Toni. So there it was on the front of that white square: "Charlie".

Later in the summer when we were sitting by the fire in Slide Canyon, I remembered all of those nice things from the beginning, those proper things, and I started laughing— couldn't stop—until Julia told me to shut up. I was hysterical. But all I could think of were things like that card. The macaroni salad I took over to dinner. The avocado seed I saved for her when I realized that while her house was clean and pretty, she didn't have any houseplants and no idea how to get any started.

Katy sat with her whiskey in front of the pages that brought the ghost of her friend onto the empty stage, making the night glow gold.

It's a long time 'til sunup, and no moon, so I've pushed aside my breakfast plate and picked up my pencil. A yellow #2 makes me feel like I am back at school with Mrs. McDonald . . . with her pretty green coat and her love for diagramming sentences . . . fussing at us boys for being boys.

Last night I dreamed that all three of the women I have loved were cooking in this kitchen. Somehow, in the dream, they all seemed to get along.

My first wife didn't teach me much about women or love or marriage. Sally just worked. She reminds me now of one of those cows who shows up with a calf year after year after year, always the same, always using the roughest parts of the country, always going out in the lead of the drive and heading straight for the corrals, like a stoic woman going for her doctor's appointment every year in May without fail. Sally was tall and thin, had skin like leather even as a young woman, woke up early and worked hard, took a shower and went to bed. She kept whatever camp and house we lived in neat and clean. She cooked meals that were plain and simple. I remember Sally standing up as soon as she finished chewing the last bite of food on her plate, standing up immediately and clearing the table, scrubbing the dishes. She didn't read books, but she made some of the most beautiful leather work I have ever seen. My main memory of her is at her leather bench, the only messy place in her life, tools and scraps spread out around her, that distinctive smell of wet leather, ready to stamp, and Sally bent over, intent on her work like I never saw her intent on anything else. I still have a pair of chaps she made me.

I can't remember having sex with Sally, no matter how hard I flip through the pages of my memory. I don't remember how she looked under my hands or at our wedding or coming from the shower wrapped in a towel. I remember the mangled wreck of our truck after she rolled it in the bar ditch. I remember how the flowers looked on her coffin. I remember how I stayed at the barn while her sister-in-law and mother gathered up all of her clothing and personal items and hauled them away.

The saddest thing is that I don't remember loving Sally.

She was just a cowboy's daughter, on the right ranch, at the right time, the right age when I got the itch to try married life. I remember being happy to have her on my arm, but truly scared of making the step that seemed so very final. I sat on my bed in the bunkhouse and sweated and got all sick to my stomach, considering whether or not to ask that girl to marry me. She was so pretty, and her quiet ways made me feel like a clumsy fool. When I spoke to her father, he looked at me hard and long, but he left the decision up to her. She said yes, of course, but now I wonder why because I don't remember us acting like we were in love or anything.

Somewhere in there I asked an older man, a good friend at the time, why it was that people got married. His answer stayed with me much longer than my memory of the actual wedding. He said, "People get married because they want someone to witness their lives, someone who thinks they are great, someone who loves them for the same reasons they love themselves. But, son, it rarely works out quite like that." I didn't understand. I was thinking about a camp job and babies. It never ceases to amaze me what wisdom passes our way without our timely recognition.

Only the other day I opened a kitchen drawer and found a mouse nest, one of my kitchen rags shredded into a hollow, all ready for babies. It made me think of how we can't escape biology. The urge to nest and reproduce is as strong in humans as in any other species, though with the human animal the heart and head get all mixed in with the process. When I first started dating Sally, she told me that she'd have my babies, and that drew me like nothing else could have. Funny how things work out. At the time I thought marrying Sally was final. It wasn't. At the time I wanted children, and I ended up, here at the end of my life, having no natural children, though I have a lot of children in my heart.

For young men, back then, there was also the idea of sleeping in a marriage bed. That looks strange on the page, maybe a little old-fashioned. Certainly naïve. I had the same thought a lot of young men had, that married men had it good. Right there beside them was a real, live, breathing woman. Not one they hoped would kiss them before the revelry in town was over. Not one who might or might not let them touch her in her soft places. But, a wife was one that they could touch and kiss whenever they pleased! Right there at the camp, at the end of the dirt road. What did we know about intimacy, bad breath, bad days, bad moods, complicated expectations, more complicated nightgowns that could plumb befuzzle a man who just wanted a little lovin' before he rolled over to sleep after a long day?

Actual marriage wasn't so much of a shock as it was an anti-climax. All of my fantasies had taken me up to "the day," or to be honest, "the night," but not much beyond that. I imagine it's the same for a lot of young men, or used to be when a couple waited until the wedding night to know each other in that way.

After we got married, I remember working harder and worrying more and being bewildered by a lot of things. I remember taking my boots off on the porch even when they weren't muddy and not passing gas even when I wanted to. I remember feeling like a stranger in my own house and especially in my own bed. Sally didn't ride a horse nor drive a vehicle when we met. She'd led a pretty sheltered life as the only girl in a family with four boys. I remember with shame the times I yelled at her while I taught her to drive the ranch truck on the dirt roads. Sally tried so hard, but all she really knew how to do was work. Now that I look back, I wish I had shown her how to have a little fun. But I didn't even know how to do that myself. I had to meet Anna for those particular lessons in my life.

Anna. Even now I have a hard time thinking about Anna without missing her, even now when I count her as my very best friend, even now when she has forgiven me, and I have forgiven myself. She is one of the biggest blessings in my life.

Anna was not my second wife. Anna ~~was~~ is the love of my life.

Katy stopped reading to touch the sentence she had just read where the word "was" had been crossed out and the word "is" written above it. She touched that sentence with wonder, with the wonder of a woman who doesn't know if anyone will ever consider her the love of his life.

My second wife, Hope, swears that I never got over Anna, that my memories of Anna kept me from truly loving again. That is one of the problems with Hope. She has a disconcerting habit of being right most of the time. And she is right about Anna. I've never gotten over her.

Anna was fun and smart and she matched me. Unlike the young man who married Sally, I didn't fall in love with Anna so she would wash my clothes or make fruit pies or have my babies. She loved doing the same things I did, for the most part, and we laughed at the same jokes. I fell in love with Anna because she was Anna.

I keep using past tense to write about her, but that is because I am writing about the Anna I knew then, the Anna I remember from when we were young, the Anna from long ago, the Anna who was always playing around with strange spices and combinations, never following a recipe the same way twice. The one who grew acres of vegetables with little effort, read piles of books by osmosis, could have calmed a hurricane with her touch, could find an arrowhead by instinct, and made me laugh with just her eyes. Anna healed things. She healed me.

There are people who always seem to be trying not to make a very big footprint. Anna was like that. It seemed like she was always trying to sneak into and out of a room without being noticed, as if she were standing sideways, sucking in her stomach so as not to make a very big shadow, as if she were determined to swim through the world without making a ripple, as if she wouldn't have breathed a breath if she thought someone else needed it, as if she were stealing a ride on life. Like one of those tiny blue butterflies that swarm the puddles in the summertime, Anna never did tread down hard enough to leave her footprint in the mud. But, there are two places where she left huge, deep, lasting prints . . . on my heart and in my memory.

I remember everything about Anna, her smell, her taste, the way she fell out of her chair at the breakfast table one morning, laughing. She is the only woman I ever laughed with in bed. She's the only woman I ever wanted to look right in the eye when we made love. There was something spiritual about loving Anna, about joining with her, which took it up above the sex thing and into something of the heart.

I remember how the bathroom smelled after her shower and what her skin felt like under my hands, how she sweated while she slept in the summer, and wrapped herself in a blanket when it was cold. I remember how nervous she made me when she drove and what a mixture of woman and child she was. She was all woman when it came to loving, all woman when it came to decisions and money and work. But she was such a child when it came to hurting, or finding something new out in nature, or believing the best about people. I remember how her fingernails were shaped and how she couldn't whistle loud enough to get the horses to come in to feed. How if she ever started laughing, she couldn't whistle at all. How she clambered over rocks and cactus and through the brush, always on a mission to find something interesting, like nature was one of those word-search puzzles and she was finding every word.

I don't have one thing that was Sally's still in my life besides those chaps she made, but Anna's presence is everywhere. The first time Hope came to my house at headquarters when we were courting, she threw a wall-eyed fit about all of Anna's stuff scattered around. It was as if Anna was so much a part of my life that I didn't notice the little marks she had made in my physical world because of the big hole her absence had left. Ironically, Hope is all about stuff, and Anna never cared about anything found in a store or in the mall. To keep peace, I packed up the nests, the rocks, the feathers, the arrowheads, the notebooks of pressed wildflowers, the whole array of lichens on rocks and bark, the field guides, the poetry. I packed up her coffee cup, the white shirt I loaned her that was too big so that she rolled up the sleeves and after five days of working cattle the insides of the cuffs were stained brown. I packed up the jar of olives from the pantry, the bag of Red Hots she never finished, a pair of panties I found pushed down to the foot of the bed after she left. Those boxes, plus her little wooden chest, lived for years in the rafters of my saddle house. When I was getting ready to move here to Cottonwood Camp, I found them stashed under the eaves where I kept my extra rolls of leather, and since I figured that Hope would never come out here, I brought them with me and unpacked them

again. I put the artifacts and treasures on the shelves I built for
Hope and that she didn't want in her house in town. I brought Anna
back into my life, not just my mailbox.

Katy stood up stiffly from the table where she had sat too
long in the pool of lamplight and grown cold. She shoved a
burled oak log into the stove and closed the damper all the way.
Instead of braving the freezing little bathroom, she brushed
her teeth at the kitchen sink, drank a long slow glass of water
to offset the whiskey toast, and crawled into her sleeping bag.
She lay looking at the glowing glass door on the stove until
she reached behind her to the old quilt folded on the back of
the couch, pulled it down over the top of her sleeping bag
and, with a strangely familiar scent up close to her face and
her head full of a woman she had never met, Katy slept.

My husband left me for Jesus. He'd tell it differently. He'd say that *he* never went anywhere. He'd say that all he did was invite Jesus into our marriage. For me it felt like a very lopsided threesome, and I wasn't interested in sharing my bed with the Son of God. From the time Mark came home from the hospital after the attack, I felt bereft, if not actually abandoned.

Mandy and Rick, my parents, are professors of art and history respectively, and I am their only child. They are hippies who peacefully protested their way through the 60s when everyone knew God was dead. It was a real eye-opener when I moved out here with Mark and discovered a whole group of people who had never heard the news, some of them ignoring this God, some of them trying to please him, some of them guilty because they couldn't. But they all knew he was there—looking down on them.

Rick says I have a dangerous habit of collecting people. I guess my experience with Charlie proved him right. I've been proving my dad's wisdom right for my whole life, and I plan on continuing that pattern as long as Rick continues being wise. I knew about Charlie a long time before I walked back behind the barn to the old boxcar where she was loading sacks of horse feed that worthless husband of hers was too lazy to come get himself. I had heard whispers of her bruises, about the "situation," but no one seemed to think it was their business to get involved. Only "somebody" should do "something." I don't know who elected me "somebody" and I never intended to do "something." I guess if I had that spring to go back and do over, I wouldn't change a thing but, damn, Rick was right. Collecting people is a dangerous, and exhilarating, habit.

People are always saying that relationships are hard work, and I've had some and seen some that were nothing but a big ol' Lassie head tilt, a whole lot of trying to speak so the other person can hear you. With those kinds of relationships, you build, one brick at a time. My marriage started out like that . . . all trying and working and looking at each other like we were from opposite hemispheres. But, there are some relationships that just explode open, blossom like a flower on fast forward. I've had two of those—and I still have them. They are my forever loves, always putting out seed, spreading new roots, surprising me with brand new flowers. Even if Uncle Bill is gone now, and Charlie didn't get exactly what she wanted, those two are still my forever loves. They are stronger and have more endurance than the other kind. I like my flowers more than I ever liked those hard-won brick walls.

Even though I am a city girl, I know about social dynamics. I understood by then that it was a big deal to have Cody Jack and Charlie over for Saturday night dinner. I understood the difference in social status and education and position between a camp man, just a cowboy, and the general manager. I am not stupid, and while I never agreed with the social structure that seems to be accepted as inevitable in rural areas, I'm not blind to it. I just chose to ignore it. I ducked my hippy-raised head, looked past the boundaries, and did what I wanted to do.

Because of the eclectic way Rick and Mandy raised me, I had never understood the phrase "culture shock." My whole life, I belonged. My parents always had a lot of friends, students, co-workers coming in and out of our house and Mandy's studio and workshop. Age or social status wasn't much of a big deal, or even sexual orientation. I made good grades, had a busy social life, and excelled at a few things in school. I had boyfriends, girlfriends, mentors. I always felt like everyone was speaking the same language. But when I moved out to the ranch, for the first time in my life I didn't belong.

All of a sudden I didn't speak the language. I encountered people who lived by rules I had no idea even existed. People who didn't measure things with the same yardstick I was accustomed to. These people talked about horses that were hands high, of land in terms of square miles, and knew to the hundredths of an inch how much rain had fallen in a particular week, month, season, or storm. They were, in my eyes and ears, sometimes grossly prejudiced or politically incorrect or narrow of thinking. Even those with deep-down goodness, who had hearts and souls of gold, had never lived outside of a four or five county area. They tried to help me, bless 'em, but I was always asking stupid questions or getting in the way.

I met Mark when he was finishing up his bachelors and I was finishing up the class work for my masters degree . . . in literature, which is impractical, I know, because I don't want to teach. I just want to read. Mark was not the usual kind of guy I was attracted to, and he was, in a way, a rebellion. But how in the world could the child of two hippies who were wildly artistic, decidedly liberal, and not even always law abiding have anything to rebel against?

It wasn't a classic rebellion like wanting a life totally opposite from my parents. To do that I'd have to move to Peachtree Road in Atlanta, Georgia, plant iris bulbs while my husband went off to run a bank. I'd go to sorority meetings while the *au pair* watched our little dear. Can you imagine? But anyway, I was sick of college, tired of the same old scene, and I wanted to show Mandy and Rick that I could do something outside the box just as well as they could. I didn't know that I was plunging right into a place full of boxes, into a place where people are supposed to fit neatly, keep their freak flags tightly furled, a place full of unwritten rules and unspoken expectations. Or at least that is how the ranch seemed to me at the beginning. I know now that people are people, no matter if they are on a college campus, in the corporate world, in the city, or way out on a ranch camp playing the fiddle to the creatures of the creek.

I am a terrible cook which is all Mandy's fault. Her idea of cooking was to visit the deli at the organic food market and lay it out pleasingly on a tray. Of course, that was before she and Rick moved onto their little thirty acres and started raising goats and digging asparagus beds, before their locavore phase. I had already left for college by that time and wasn't in on that particular re-invention of their lives the way I was the music phase or the alternative medicine phase or the embracing of the multi-media artists who moved into our basement one summer.

I married into a world where the women all cook and most of them are good cooks. Who knew I would move somewhere forty-five miles from a post office, and even further from a deli selling organic goose liver? During the first couple of weeks after our honeymoon, Mark wanted me to see the ranch so I rode around with him in the pickup, and we'd make a sandwich when we got home to headquarters. Then fall works cranked up, and he was eating at the cook shack two meals a day, but later on, when shipping was over and I was tired of bouncing around in his truck seeing the same old windmills and the same old cows on the same old rough roads, he would come in to find me reading or watching television or writing on my thesis and wonder what was for dinner. That was when he found out that I couldn't cook and I found out that he could.

He taught me a standard meal I made whenever we had guests. I wrapped potatoes in tin foil, put them in the oven, set out toppings like cheese and sour cream in a divided dish we got for a wedding gift while Mark grilled steaks outside. I made a green salad, and mixed vinaigrette from a package in a cut-glass cruet—another wedding present. I made his mother's recipe for an impressive cake that uses a yellow cake mix, Eagle Brand milk, a can of cream of coconut, and Cool Whip. That's pretty much all I could cook—until I ended up hanging out with Charlie, of course—and found out what you can make with nothing. She's like the Zen master of cooking with nothing. It was fun to learn from her. She thinks she's dumb, but she's not. She's good at a lot of things as long as they have a practical application. I am more of a dreamer, the one who's been places and read books . . . not that those travels or pages of learning did me any good when things got bad. It's a good thing both of us came together like we did last summer. If we'd never become friends, she'd still be getting black eyes and scary nights and I'd be bored spitless, listening to Mark talk about his near-death come-to-Jesus moment for the thousandth time. We'd both be dead inside. I'd have missed out on two big loves and a whole huge helping of life.

Mark was different when we first married—I mean, before he met Jesus. We had a wonderful tender courtship, and when the natural step for him was marriage, I didn't think much about it. Mandy tried to talk to me about taking my time and not making such a solid alliance right from the beginning, but Mark said that we couldn't live together out at the ranch without being married. He had to move out here to start his new job, and he thought it would look better if he brought a wife with him rather than, as he put it, ran back and forth to town to see a girlfriend who ought to love him enough to be with him. So I walked down the aisle as if it were inevitable. Looking back, I see that with the end of my grad program coming up, I was panicked . . . had no idea what to do with myself next. A marriage proposal was a life raft. Now I wonder why I didn't do more research . . . though that sounds awfully scientific and clinical, not at all poetic. But romance and poetry are overrated when you are filing divorce papers.

We spent the first six months adjusting to each other, and—for me—adjusting to life on the ranch. That seems a little backwards now, now that I know what being married means. Looks like we would have done some adjusting before saying things like 'til death do us part.

In the beginning of our marriage, morning was my favorite time. I have always liked mornings especially because Mandy doesn't and Rick does. I loved, as a little girl and later as a teenager, getting up in the quiet house that smelled of coffee and finding Rick surrounded by his books, eating toast and apricot preserves. I would join him, no conversation necessary. Mornings are a time of intimacy, a time before the purity of the day gets muddled. At the beginning we would set the alarm for an hour before Mark had to be up and play under the covers until we slid out of bed to drink coffee, and he would cook breakfast for me. We never turned the light on when we made love in the mornings, though, because Mark was afraid that someone would see the bedroom light come on, but not the kitchen light shortly thereafter, and would know what we were doing. Living at headquarters is like living in a fishbowl. All the window blinds twitch when someone starts a vehicle. Or turns on a light.

It feels odd, telling you all of this, Katy. I mean, you know some of it. Maybe all of it. I keep forgetting that you dated Mark that summer before I met him. He and I met at a friend's party. It was pretty clichéd, really, and boring. A lot of talk about finals and papers and thesis review committees, a table full of junk food and beer. I remember thinking that Mark's eyes were sad. It was several months after you two broke up, but he hadn't started dating again. Some of the women on the ranch thought I didn't know about you when we first moved out here, but of course I did. You were all Mark talked about on our first three dates. Katy Benson. One of the heirs to the Benson Ranch where he had done an internship and where he hoped to hire on as general manager after he graduated. After I met you, I understood why he fell for you, but never understood how he had hoped to hold on to you! But isn't the whole world supposed to be a mirror? Maybe I was wondering how he meant to hold on to me. And, of course, he almost didn't, which would have made this a very sad story if you think about it.

After our third date, I decided to be blunt with him. I met him at the door on our fourth date, put my finger over his lips, pushed him into a chair, sat down on his lap, traced a heart shape right on his starched shirt, and said, "This heart will never heal if you keep picking the scab off. Mark, you are going to have to stop talking about her if you want to love again, if you want to forget how she hurt you. We've got to talk about something else if I am going to keep going out with you." So we did. We talked about my thesis, about his dreams and ambitions, about my parents and their new goat farm, about books, about the Benson-Ranch-minus-mention-of-Katy-Benson. And it worked because that night he stayed over. He stopped looking so sad, and he started throwing his head back and laughing out loud. I love that sound.

But, all of our fun and morning lovemaking halted after Mark's appendix ruptured. After he met Jesus. For one thing, there was his recovery from surgery, a lot of pain and figuring out what he could and couldn't eat, what he should and shouldn't lift. Stuff like that. Later on, Mark seemed confused about what to do about Jesus *and* a hard-on for me. He began to devote his mornings to his Bible and his prayer time, and I drank coffee alone or stayed in bed.

"Appendix!" Cody Jack looked baffled. "Oh, I thought it was a bad horse wreck or something."

The two couples sat around a table covered with the remains of a steak dinner, yellow cake crumbs on the small dessert plates in front of them.

"No," Mark explained, "Many people do think it was a much more spectacular event, but it is the small things that change us, that get our attention. My appendix burst on the way to the hospital and I almost lost my life. But I found my Savior. Oh, don't get me wrong, I grew up in church, sometimes three times a week. I knew who Jesus was. Knew the stories from the Word. I knew what was right and wrong. I even, sometime in junior high when it was expected of me, walked down the aisle at church camp and shook Jesus' hand. So to speak!" Mark paused and sat back in his chair, his sweating tea glass in his hand like a stage prop. "But there in that hospital, after my life had hung in the balance and all of those people prayed me through, I got to *know* Jesus." He sat his glass down with a thump on the word know. "And that wasn't the end of it. It's not like I found my Savior and it was all just a walk in the park after that. No, there have been hard times and lots of dealings with the Lord since then." He smiled over at Julia with what she liked to call his *dewy eyes, compassionately loving the sinner* look. "Even today I am praying for my dear wife to find the same peace and love that I have found in Him. Praying even as we dine on this lovely meal she has prepared."

From mid-winter through early spring, Charlie bought boring food: macaroni, potatoes, rice, beans, canned vegetables, and bread. Their beef was furnished by the ranch and Charlie bought fruit juice in cans while from November until June she longed for vegetables, berries, melons, and the crunch of green things between her teeth. She opened jars of salsa and preserves and ate them by the spoonful, eager for the sunshine contained in each bite.

Her small truck rattled along the dusty road, pushed hard by the wind that moved soil from one still-brown pasture to the next. Paper sacks rattled in the seat beside her. There were not very many of them because her grocery budget had been smashed, yet again, by the hot checks Cody Jack wrote when she wasn't paying attention. The sacks contained inexpensive, almost imitation, foods, four rolls of cheap toilet paper, and one item that she thought of over and over as she drove the eleven miles of dirt out to Live Oak Camp on the 3R.

After the meal at Julia and Mark's, Charlie had started rooting cuttings of her house plants in jars to give to Julia. Today, as a bonus, she had bought an avocado, one avocado, a whole dollar fifty for that one fruit, so that in the center of the crate of cuttings she could place the seed, poked by toothpicks, its bottom resting in water. When she was almost home, Charlie ground the truck to a stop, rustled in the brown sacks until she came up with the green-black fruit. She scored it all the way around lengthwise with her pocket knife, twisted the halves apart, carefully thwacked her knife blade into the exposed seed, and turned the blade until the seed lifted from the green meat. She put the seed into one of the sacks and then sliced each half of the fruit in half again, peeled back the black skin, and stuffed each quarter into her mouth, no salt, no mayo, no hot sauce, nothing to mask the taste of that green. The exotic flesh slid down her throat, and tears of desire wet her eyes.

I will always feel guilty for eating that avocado because if you really love someone, you want to give them everything, give them all the good things, the best things. I should have given it to Julia whole and just explained how to root the seed.

When I told Cody Jack we had dinner plans on Friday night over to Julia and Mark's, he started to protest but then changed his mind. He even waited to have his first beer until after noon that day. He took a shower and wore his good hat. He griped, saying he wished he had known in advance so as to get a new pair of boots, but we both knew there was no money for such nonsense. He was only looking for something to gripe about anyways. All in all, he was on his best behavior that night, and really for the next few months when he saw the friendship between me and Julia. Cody Jack isn't stupid— just mean.

I know he had a real hard childhood, that his dad was a rough old man who ran most of his kids off by the time they were thirteen or fourteen. His mom was an alcoholic, I think, and left about the time Cody Jack did. When a kid is raised mean and unloved, he spends a lot of his life looking for good feelings. Like Cody, always looking for more sleep, more food, more alcohol, more jokes, more highs, more sex, more ways of making someone else feel worse than him. Uncle Bill said maybe Cody Jack had "never enough" syndrome. I don't know about any syndrome, but I do think that the problem with people like that is that they don't ever get enough, and

49

it just plumb burns them up inside, and sometimes they take other people with them.

I've always heard about men who would hit a woman and then be sorry, buying flowers and stuff to make up for it, crying and begging the woman to forgive them. I've heard about how hard it was for the woman to break the pattern because the man was so sweet between times, and how she really loved him after all. That sure wasn't the deal with Cody Jack. Even when he wasn't hitting something, like when he was around the boss or people he wanted to like him, his mean was right there below the surface. Like when he was shoeing a horse. Sometimes, all it took was for the horse to jerk his foot away once for the mean to spill all over everything. Cody Jack would hit him again and again with a rasp or the claw end of the hammer. I never knew if I wanted to be there when he was shoeing to try to make him stop hurting the horse, or wanted to be far, far away so I didn't have to see, so I didn't have to know.

Those are the kinds of things Julia didn't understand when we first met.

Mark was outside by the grill when we got to Benson Ranch headquarters, and I took the macaroni salad on into the house. I don't know what it was about going to someone's house that made me feel all grown up. I mean, real going to dinner where there is real food all thought out beforehand instead of just a bunch of people saying, "Hey, let's cook a steak," which really means, "Let's get drunk so someone can fight and we'll either let the girls drive home or pass out on the living room floor." It's no wonder some of the wives around here drink. It's self-defense.

The thing about feeling all grown up is that once you really do grow up you wonder why you wanted to. That's how I felt later that summer, wondering what the fuss was about—being a grown up only made me feel tired. I thought I'd feel like a grown up the first time I ever had sex. But it's awkward, isn't it? Maybe not everyone feels silly. Embarrassed. Yucky. I remember the next morning I was scared and ashamed. I never did it again until I got with Cody Jack—and then it wasn't a big deal—seemed like just another chore that had to get done. Cody Jack kept an economy-sized bottle of baby oil beside the bed. I hate the smell of baby oil.

We didn't talk about sex the first time we hung out, Julia and me. She chattered about not being a good cook, about how Mark wanted a baby and she wasn't sure, about wanting to plant a garden and all. I told her about my horses, my dogs, my cats, even doing a silly imitation of the one with the broken-backed crooked walk. That was the first time I ever made her laugh.

We washed up the dishes when the guys were done eating and went out to sit on the porch with two longneck beers Julia snuck from beneath the lettuce in the bottom drawer of her fridge. It made me laugh on the inside when I thought it was probably killing Cody Jack not to have a beer as he sat all stiff on the couch talking to Mark. Or rather, Mark was talking. Julia and I didn't sit on the porch chairs. Instead we plopped down on the top of the steps. When I pointed out that the moon was waxing, about half-way to full, she reached out her hand and touched my hair. Then she said, "You pay attention to the moon, too, huh?"

51

The little house was gray and the sky all around was still dark. Katy shivered as she crammed the stove with the remainder of the stacked wood and blew hard on the coals. Since she was already frozen, she put on her shoes and went out to the woodpile, filling her arms with as much as she could carry. The crash of the split logs to the hearth was rude in the dawn quiet. Katy wasn't usually an early riser, but something about being on the ranch snagged her out of sleep and off the couch.

She opened the door to the bathroom and started the hot water running into the tub while she burned her fingers lighting the little wall heater with a wooden strike-anywhere match. As the tub filled, she fixed the coffee pot at the kitchen sink and plugged it in beside the table. She bathed with the door to the bathroom wide open. The smell of coffee mingling with wood smoke made her groan as she lay back in the hot water.

Katy was familiar with limbo. It was as if life had taught her to float, but she'd never learned to swim. From the time her parents had separated until she graduated from high school, she had floated between them, between two bedrooms, a bedroom at Dad's house, a bedroom at Mom's. Then she expanded her float to include a shabby, messy, busy, chaotic apartment close to the college campus. Somewhere in there, in an effort to embrace her family heritage, to understand why she bore her mother's last name rather than her father's, she had started spending time out on the Benson Ranch. By then her Uncle Richard was dead and her mother was very ill. Katy couldn't stand the smell of the chemicals oozing from her mother's skin or the sight of her bald head. Going out to the ranch was a kind of penance, an acknowledgement of her place in the line of heirs. And it was an escape. To her surprise, it also was a place of joy and pleasure all stirred up with work.

After years of a kind of backpacker existence, never feeling truly settled anywhere, she made a nest almost by accident. The summer she spent working at the ranch she slept in the bedroom beside the cavernous kitchen of the Big House. One restless night she wandered through the various rooms that bore the marks of an interior decorator hired some thirty years before. As she prowled, she began picking things up. A Navajo rug, a Mexican basket, a bronze of a cowboy leaning against his horse's shoulder. Before long, she was scouring the house with intent, carting the things she liked the most into her bedroom. She traded the painting above the bed, one showing two mountain men shooting a grizzly, for one of brown-skinned women grinding corn side by side, the sun setting behind them. She moved books around, filling the shelves in the room with titles she already loved and volumes that looked like ones she'd come to love someday. She drug a heavy overstuffed chair into one corner and traded the boring desk for a cunning, old-fashioned secretary from another bedroom. She created the first haven of her life.

It had been embarrassing when the housekeeper, the mechanic's wife, had reported paintings and artwork "stolen" from the Big House. She'd had to confess to doing some rearranging, but for the first time she felt a sense of home. She almost wished for a magic wand to disappear the rest of the house, leaving her with the old-fashioned red-trimmed kitchen with its sturdy cooking utensils and her own little suite. The next time she was in the city, she bought sheets, towels, leather-scented candles and a toothbrush that she left in the holder beside the sink. Mark never slept there when they were having their romance.

When she graduated from college, freshly grieving her mother's death, she closed and locked the door to that little room, stashed the bulk of her belongings in her best friend's apartment, and fled overseas with her camera. She went back to camping again, sometimes literally living out of the pack on her back. If she had been bluntly honest with herself, she would have said she was looking for love, perhaps even looking for herself, definitely looking for something to believe in. Somewhere along the way, she found those things. She found a love for every face she photographed: young, old, male, female, looking the camera in the eye, or intent on living, not even realizing the camera was there. She fell in love with every tree, every river, every mountain peak, every narrow street, every flavor, every smell. She fell in love with the self she found along the way, the self she saw reflected in the eyes of the people from many countries, many backgrounds, and in many moods. Since returning from Europe, she had been living in the city with her best friend and two other girls, making a stab at editing and selling photographs, possibly writing a book, her bags and boxes still packed around her, still unplanted.

Now, soaking in Uncle Bill's tub, in Uncle Bill's house, she realized that she had come home, that regardless of the story on the kitchen table, she had been coming home to the Benson Ranch all along.

When the water cooled, Katy dried off and dressed in a much bigger hurry than she had gotten undressed. The glowing woodstove, the smell of coffee, and the thought of those yellow pages pulled her into the day. She dumped last night's cold tea down the sink, and by the time she had finished her first cup of coffee, she was halfway through a bowl of oatmeal with brown sugar and lots of butter. As she ate, she turned the fragile pages of the little book from beside Bill's bed.

Give me mud,
heavy black fragrant,
goldfish harbor
at the bottom of the trough.

If I ever find the perfect stick for digging wild onions,
I am going to keep it forever.
I will leave it to my daughter who will find it among my things,
and sigh,
and wonder about her weird mother.
Or perhaps she will put it in her panty drawer
and some spring
will go out to hunt for tiny purple flowers that wave above the
rocks and grasses
in the April wind.

After Katy folded her sleeping bag and washed her dishes, she wrapped Bill's pottery coffee mug in a worn dish towel and carried it in to the old wooden box in the bedroom. As she passed back by the shelves along the wall of the living room, she paused and touched some of the items along their length: a mano that fit into her palm perfectly, a basket of crude pottery sherds, a piece of layered orange sandstone, a lichen-covered chunk of wood, a beetle's carcass, its promise of shining green showing through the thin film of dust, a cunning bird nest shaped like a hanging basket. Out of curiosity, she knelt on the floor and lifted the olla from its place. Her olla. She traced the places where the pottery had been glued back together, saw the faint brushstrokes that had faded to a muted gray on the red clay. Resting in its belly were the postcards and photographs she had sent to Bill Morgan over the past few years. At the end of the shelves, on the wall beside the bathroom door, somewhat hidden from the rest of the room, she saw the framed portrait she had made of him three years earlier and hung there herself. The image showed Uncle Bill standing on the porch as the sun went down, his fiddle cradled like a lover beneath his chin. He wasn't looking toward the camera, but rather way off up the canyon, deep shadows in the creases of his face. Katy heard the songs from that evening, the songs from that fiddle, the songs from that man.

She poured a third cup of coffee and settled in to where the yellow legal pads lay waiting. The sun was full up.

I grew up on a small ranch, more of a farm really. My childhood was nothing special, and, in its ordinariness, very special. I grew up like a lot of kids did, working hard, playing hard, being loved hard, being dismissed by the big folks and hazed by my peers. I learned a lot from my pa and my uncles, was loved a lot by my ma. I smoked behind the barn with my boy cousins, drank too much moonshine about the time I was sixteen and puked my guts up. I swam in the creek in the summertime, kissed a girl after a country dance, went to school, and forgot to go to college.

I had a few good teachers, lots of mediocre ones, a handful of lousy ones, and a couple of great ones. I had a big crush on one of those mediocre teachers when I was in high school, and she let me touch her hair once, when no one was looking. Now, I think maybe she was a little bit sweet on me, too.

When I was a young man, I made a big circle away from the country where I grew up, determined not to be a home guard cowboy like my dad and my older brother. That circle led me through New Mexico, Texas, some into Montana and Wyoming, though I didn't stay long in that north country. I spent some time on the prairie where the land is rich and productive, but the circle of nothing around me was too big. I did a little stint in Utah but missed the culture where the chilies are hot and the women are dark-eyed and shy. I ended up circling back around to this place where the water and rocks and trees blend in with the desert. I spent those early years on big outfits and small outfits, but once I settled here, well, it's been hard to imagine going anywhere else. I went back home to visit every so often until there wasn't anyone left to visit.

Like a lot of lifetime cowpunchers, my life has been a job, a job that defined me, a job that dictated what I wore and where I lived, certainly who and what I have loved. I've ridden a lot of horses that were just horses, and two really great ones, one retired right here on this camp—that old Jasper horse. Sorry old cuss, almost completely blind and no teeth left. I had a couple of fine mentors along the way. I've had several great friends, most of 'em gone now.

I have always wanted to be out of doors, under a big sky, doing something physical with a measure of independence. Like a lot of young men, I was drawn to this job because it could be done from the back of a horse. At the beginning, the cows were, in a way, incidental. And I do admit that I still like nothing more than a good mount. But, the older I get, the more I like cows. I like how they move, how they form social units, how they chew their cud, how they use the land. I like working with cows. I like seeing the baby calves, how steers and bulls go through a gawky awkward phase just like teenage boys. I like seeing heifers in the same social unit as their mamas. They understand family, you know. A cow's whole life is structured around the mother/child relationship. She hangs out with her friends, eats, walks to water or salt, always with her baby by her side. When it is hot, she lies down under a tree with her calf and takes a nap. It isn't a bad way to organize your life if you think about it.

Cows are smart. They know where the good water can be found, know what to eat and what to leave alone. They make up their minds to like a fella, or not, in the first few moments of contact.

I enjoy seeing the same cow with a new calf, year after year, or maybe I'll see that same cow some year with a big bag and realize that a lion got her calf. That causes me a grief that is fresh and sharp and real. The philosophers call this anthropomorphism, and so be it. Most cowhands would say that I am a sentimental fool gone soft with age. So be that, too.

Sally and I had lived on three different outfits before she died, and I had already talked to Benson on the phone, already agreed to go to work for him when she rolled that truck in the ditch. Like a lot of young men, I was pretty fiddle-footed back then, always searching for the perfect ranch job, thinking that one outfit was going to treat me better than another. Sally, bless her heart, followed right along. When I say that we were on our way to work for Benson, I mean that our boxes were packed and our mail forwarded. We were set to pull out the next morning.

I don't remember much about the day Sally died or the days immediately afterward, don't much remember deciding to go ahead and come on out here. Sally's mother and some of the other ranch women unpacked and repacked the boxes she had taped shut, removing her personal belongings. I think they were being kind, trying to spare my feelings. What they didn't know was that when I moved to South Camp alone, I put most of those boxes in the back room and shut the door. I rolled my bedroll out on top of the bedstead and used my tin camp outfit in the kitchen. I didn't bother with the whole household for a couple of years, only gradually bringing things out of that back room as I had a need for them.

After Sally died, my throat got all tight. The only things I could swallow with ease were coffee and whiskey. It made for a long year, or couple years, I forget. What saved me was the job, the land, the love of living at South Camp. And Richard Benson. He must have *known what I needed, and that was a whole lot of time and space and hard work.*

And books. Books probably saved me more than anything else. A man can't be too lonely when he reads. And reading made something more of me, I'd like to believe. Made me more of a thinker. I don't know if that is good or bad, if it makes a man more content or less, more settled or less, more able to see clearly or less. But the truth is that reading filled those years for me.

Once a month I would go into town to one of those big bookstores and buy a stack of magazines and books. I wasn't spending my money on anything else besides whiskey and what few groceries I couldn't get from the commissary at headquarters. I liked picking out magazines that were so far removed from the dirt and sweat and realness of my life that it was as if they were published on a different planet. If I liked one, I would make a note of it and buy it again the next month. I bought magazines full of national and world news, horses, vehicle mechanics, naked women, essays, fiction, puzzles, photography, travel, cartoons, and sometimes a woman's magazine full of makeup, hairstyles, and recipes.

I got clued in to what books I had missed out on and what new ones I wanted to read, going on sprees where I read everything an author had written. The best of those books I kept, and they are here in this house, except a few that Hope put in a box and stuck in the garage. They got water damaged and I had to throw them out.

I learned what good writing is, not that I will ever be able to duplicate it. I learned that I may never know what makes a poem a poem. I learned to think globally, in terms of this planet and humanity as a whole rather than just this ranch or people that don't touch each other.

I learned that not every woman has an orgasm. At least not when she's with a man. I started paying attention after that, you can be sure. I watched all the women I knew and speculated about which category they fell into: never, only alone, with a lot of work, or always. Shameful sport, and it's a good thing I don't intend to show these pages to anyone. The most painful tears I cried over Sally were months after she died. I cried because I didn't know which category she fit into, and damn it, I should have. Of all people, I should have known.

Hope fit into the sometimes with a lot of work category, but Anna was an always gal, the most giving and sweetest woman in bed I have ever known, receptive and open and as eager to be pleased as she was to please. She was ready for love, and I know I was too, at that point.

"You old goat!"

Katy's laughter rang out over the camp, ran down the creek, and bounced off of granite rock. Uncle Bill had placed a small star beside the paragraph, but the note in the margin was only one character. A question mark.

She had moved onto the porch as the day warmed and began to feel like spring for sure, scooting her chair around with the sun. Still grinning, Katy got up from her patch of sunshine and went inside where she made a sandwich and washed some grapes. When she came back out with her lunch, she sat on the porch swing. No book. No music. No company. She pushed the swing with one foot and ate, staring off at the hills, breathing and swinging. For once in her life, Katy Benson was still.

These yellow pages are a little hateful to me sometimes. They keep filling up and I haven't written anything about the story I want to tell. And, lately, I am not sure that my part of the story, the part that only I know about, is that important.

I dreamed of Anna again last night. I dreamed we were swimming in water where there was no shore. In the dream, I was nervous, agitated, unsure of what was lurking beneath my feet or where we were headed or what lay in store for us. But not Anna. She was like a mermaid or a fish, paddling tirelessly around me, always laughing, her eyes glowing above the waves.

I met Anna soon after the southern half of this ranch went up for sale. I had been at the camp for over a month and decided I couldn't put off going to town any longer. Richard Benson had been struggling financially for a number of years and, after all of his meetings with bankers and realtors, he finally decided that the only way to hold on to at least a part of his father's and his uncle's dream was to split it up. That was a sad time. When I drove through headquarters, Benson was standing on the porch waiting for me. I never did get to town that day. We went into his office, and before he got well into his story, we were well into a bottle. It seems bad news and drinking go together. For Benson, the hardest part was the idea that he was letting two old dead men down. For me, it was the prospect of having to leave South Camp. By the time the sun set, we were fuzzy with bourbon. He pulled out a map of the ranch and we leaned over it while he asked me to take over the southern half and, when it sold, count the cattle over to the new owner and then come north to continue on as Benson Ranch foreman. It seemed like such an opportunity at the time, though over the next few years I began to see that opportunity a little differently than I did the night the bottle passed between us. It took awhile to get the property on the market, over a year for the ranch to actually sell, and then near onto two years for the transition to be made. We had a lot of wild cattle in those days.

Anyway, as soon as the ranch actually went on the market, I moved from South Camp up to the camp right on the highway. It was then I started going into town more often. I missed the more remote camp, but it was nice to be able to eat someone else's cooking once in awhile. Anna was working at the Dairy Queen, and after the first time I saw her, I started driving in every few nights. I'd order a burger, fries, and iced tea, and listen to Anna work while I ate.

Something about Anna relaxed me. I would watch her wipe down a table or lean over the counter to hand an ice cream to a child, her feet swinging off the floor because she was totally in the moment, and all of my tension and loneliness would drain away. It became a habit, this practice of going in to eat and listen to that girl trying to learn Spanish from the cooks in the back, this habit of having my arm branded with her touch until the next time I walked through the door and into her space.

Most men, me included, think in terms of body parts when they think of a woman, at least in the darkest part of our minds where we are most honest. A tiny waist, soft shiny hair, big or small breasts—a cliché—the perfect or imperfect woman. And true to form, I thought of Anna in pieces, but it was pieces like her eyes that could tell a whole story or absorb a whole story. Or her hair that never did exactly what she wanted it to. Or her hands that could soothe the devil's toothache. I thought of Anna as a laugh, a silly little dance when she was happy, and—later—as the mole that rested on her left hip bone, the fine downy hairs on her arms, the crooked little toe on her right foot, and the way she shied from my presence if I ever got angry. If I ever got mad or raised my voice, that girl would evaporate like so much smoke, just be gone. Once I slammed my fist on the table at dinner, ranting about something that had nothing to do with her, and I saw a look on her face that haunts me, especially now that I know her whole story.

One night I hung around until closing time, stayed as Anna turned the sign around on the door, listened to the click of the lock, smelled the mop water as it swished across the floor. When she was finished, I held out my hand and she put hers in it. We went out to my truck and she climbed in. I cupped her face in my hands and kissed her. Then I asked her to move out to the ranch with me and she said yes. Two nights later, when I drove up, she had her belongings stashed in the back room of the Dairy Queen, tied up in garbage sacks. I threw them in the back of the truck and that was that. It was like a fairy tale. When I told Benson, he barely believed me. I barely believe it myself, even now.

Anna and I didn't make love the first night we were together all those years ago. After she crawled up into the cab beside me, she shoved whatever stuff I had in the middle of the seat over to the passenger side and settled herself where she rode from then on, right next to me, her leg next to mine, her hand on my thigh. Even in the ranch truck, when it meant clambering over fencing pliers, odd gloves, sulfur boluses, and a water jug to open the gates, she still plopped herself right by my side, the gear shift between her knees. Our days were tailored around work, but because everything on the ranch was new to her, it became new for me, too. Every bird, every rock formation, every frog in a slot canyon, every cactus fruit, every squirrel, every water hole, every change in the weather was special to Anna. She delighted in everything. And no matter what I was doing, there she was, learning, helping, getting in the way, lifting her end, wanting to be there, and she was so much there that when she wasn't anymore, there was a big hole in my life.

When we left the Dairy Queen parking lot that night, she was like a glowing lantern, but the closer we got to the camp the dimmer and dimmer she shone. I've read about energy, potential and kinetic, and it was as if both kinds seeped out of her. She was very still, even as we walked into the house. As if she had left me altogether—already.

I did the right thing, one of the few times I can look back on and think so. I pulled some blankets out of the closet, put them on the couch for her, and brought her a pillow from my bed. She took off her shoes slowly, and when I offered to unload her belongings, she shook her head. In all of her clothes, she curled up under the blankets, only her eyes visible. I poured us both a drink, cheap whiskey probably, and sat on the floor beside the couch. Our only contact was the clink of her glass against mine when I said, "To beginnings." She drank long and deep, one tear that I pretended not to see sliding down onto the pillowcase.

In the middle of the night, she crept into my bed, dragging the pillow in with her. She had taken off her jeans but still had on her shirt. I didn't do anything but open my arms, wrap her up tight, and we both slept. It was the only night we spent together with clothes on.

Anna always said that when you really love someone, you want them to have the biggest piece of chocolate cake. And I wanted to give that girl the best of everything, so I guess she was right.

The trash bags we had loaded into the back of my truck stayed tied shut, for the most part, for many weeks. Little by little, it seemed, Anna made a physical mark on my life, but she was careful, oh so careful, not to bother anything, even when I would have liked for her to bother things a little bit. But without meaning to, Anna became so much a part of my world that it wasn't until she left that I noticed how many things she had moved into my space. Well, not "things" so much as ways. Sure, I ended up with shelves full of nature stuff, some books, her treasures, but also her laugh, her incessant humming, the way she turned her back to strip off her jeans when we went swimming or were getting ready for bed, as if maybe she wasn't so revealed if she couldn't see me.

I loved waking up, that first morning, and every morning, with her in my arms. She always gave to life more than she demanded from it. I feel like I spent four years basking in Anna. We woke up reaching out hands for each other if we were not already tangled up, limbs and breath. We usually got out of bed laughing. Anna used to say that I didn't like being awake if she wasn't awake, too, and that if I woke up, I always woke her up, too. I don't know if that is completely true, because I do remember watching her sleep while the room turned from navy blue to gray, but maybe it is a little true, because I liked watching her eyes come open and her window on the world light up. Going from making love all the time, with eyes, hands, mouth, with clothes on, with clothes off, with words, with smiles, noisy, silent, with great intimacy, and even with our hearts in public, to making love with Hope once a week in a sedate manner, was quite a contrast. It wasn't like apples and oranges. More like oranges and pinecones.

I learned from Anna. When she would jump out and open a wire gate, let me drive through, and then shut it again with herself on the wrong side, she would look all surprised and then do a little clown dance, making fun of herself, laughing at her own clumsiness. She was as apt to find a mushroom growing under the bark of a dead tree as she was to see a herd of deer or spot the cow we were trailing. Even when we were mucking around the barn, she was delighted— over a litter of kittens in the hay, an old mason jar full of horsehair, a moth wing, a coon track in the loose dirt, a bat hanging from the rafters of the machine shed.

Once, when we were riding fence, we found a cave. Inside the cave was an almost-whole olla, mainly the deep bottom and some of the sides, one of them all the way up to the rounded lip. Anna gathered the pieces and wrapped them carefully in handkerchiefs and my white cotton T-shirt. She took care of them the rest of the day, riding with the biggest piece in her lap, the rest tucked into a saddle bag. She spent a week piecing those sherds back together and *gluing them in place. The finished pot grew steadily on a piece of newspaper. It is one of my greatest treasures.*

Katy gathered up the pieces of her nest out on the porch and moved back into the house. Though spring had arrived, she knew that a fire would be welcome and comforting in the evening. But out of the wind, the puddle of late afternoon sunlight turned the kitchen table into the perfect reading spot.

We had the whole southern part of the ranch to ourselves. That was a very busy time in my life, but Anna went along as if that was exactly what she was supposed to do. She was always right behind me or right beside me, right where she wanted to be. I think. I hope, anyway. Those months were like a dream, just the two of us, living at the camp on the highway, the one they turned into the 3R headquarters later on. When we could, we would trot off to South Camp for days on end, using whatever excuse presented itself. The world went on without us. That was a fine time for me. I had been alone for so long, and all of a sudden there was Anna, being so careful not to make waves in my life, careful even about where she put her toothbrush, and adapting to all of my bachelor ways, never putting the big frying pan on the little frying pan nail, as the old expression goes. The world "halcyon" is a little dramatic, maybe even affected, but I always think it when I think of that time.

We swam in the deep parts of the creek. We made popcorn and read books in front of the fire. We played cards with wagers that became more and more outrageous as time went on, more and more hilarious, at least to us. We threw snowballs. We cooked meals in tandem, sometimes walking and talking all over each other. We held hands. We made "Sunday dates" that meant breakfast in bed with books, movies, and never getting dressed, though days with no work were few during those years. What I really miss about Anna is that she made work fun for me. When I had a horse to shoe, Anna was there with a water jug and conversation. When I went to clean out a water trough, there was Anna with a shovel, stopping now and again to examine a bug or insist that I kiss her. I loved our days, loved our mornings, loved our nights—but it was our evenings that meant the most to me. We would unsaddle, drink a beer on the porch or on the couch, decide what to cook together for dinner, totally immerse ourselves in each other, talk about the work we did that day. Anna loved a hot bath, coming out of the bathroom all glowing and clean. In the winter, she would take her bath early and then we'd curl up on the couch and it was like having a warm little rabbit beside me. We read books, played cards, talked, drank, and many, many nights I sawed on the fiddle while she listened or pretended to read. Sometimes I never knew how we got from the living room to the bed . . . it was just a natural flow. We found ourselves in each other's arms, and woke up that way, too.

It was my responsibility to turn the 3R over to the new owners in the best possible shape. We built fence and did projects that no one but me will ever know about or appreciate. I tried to catch every flaw, every fault that a new owner would see. In hindsight, I probably stressed about it much more than was entirely necessary. After all, it has changed hands twice since then. But we are who *we are, and I am glad that during that time I had Anna. With her I could worry out loud, and it was as if those worries turned into smoke and blew away on the breeze. With Anna, I could talk about the things I had read, things that had been stuck in my head for a long time, and she would come back with something I hadn't thought of. I would not have admitted to loneliness before Anna came to live with me. Now I see that not only was I lonely before that time, but I have been a little bit lonely ever since.*

I had been alone as a young man on various cow camps, stayed pretty much alone even after I got married, had been alone again for a long time after Sally died. People ask me how I did it then, how I do it now, and the truth is that it is easy for me to live alone. I like books. I like animals. I like being out of doors, out in the weather for days on end. I like music and learned to play the fiddle to give myself that gift, the gift of music. I do things to please myself, do things because I stand in judgment of myself. I find solace in precision— don't need a witness for small acts or big ones.

The bad thing is that I also suffer from the same disease everyone does once they have been alone too long. I tend to talk too much when I do get around people after a series of days or weeks of solitude. I start wishing for the sound of my own voice being absorbed by someone else's eardrums. I often find that ideas that make perfect sense rattling around inside my own head look ridiculous when they are held up against the reactions on another person's face.

When I am living alone, as I am now, I keep things simple. Wear the same clothes day after day. Play the same three bars on the fiddle, over and over again, eat the same meal four days in a row, talk to myself, letting the sounds of my ideas become poems. I go to bed when I am tired, make as much noise early in the morning as I want, use all the hot water, and sing old silly songs out loud when I think of them. I eat peaches straight out of the can and drink the juice.

The pack mule's load was lighter, but the old man's heart was heavier as he rode up out of Slide Canyon. He'd left a package of good steaks and other items to help Charlie and Julia make their last few hours of camping more fun. His mind was at ease, having found them, having seen that—for the most part—they were doing okay, with a few bruises and a pretty scary story to tell. He was proud of Charlie for the way the camp looked and for how she had closed up the cut on Julia's head. Mixed in with the positive was the sure knowledge that they all had some heartache still coming their way.

He knew it was foolish, riding all the way back to Cottonwood just to give the girls one more night of peace. He had seen in Julia's eyes a desire to get back to creature comforts, get back and see what had become of the life she'd left behind, and at the same time, a reluctance to face reality. She had walked down to the swimming hole while he and Charlie sat under the tree and talked. When Julia slipped off her jeans and slipped into the cold spring water, Bill wished he could help Charlie get rid of the look on her face—the one of adoration—as she watched Julia swim. He tried to distract her by asking about her gun and if she had seen signs of anyone else around.

Bill Morgan rode toward home full of an anger, a horror, a sorrow, a guilt, a whole handful of questions about what was coming next. Reading the story on the ground was a lifelong habit, so when a fresh and unfamiliar set of horse tracks cut from the bushes half a mile from Cottonwood Camp, cut onto the trail in front of him, Uncle Bill was certain that the next chapter of the story was about to begin.

Julia was used to the pews by now, used to the order of the service, recognized several familiar faces in the congregation. She even knew some of the songs and found herself singing or humming along. Tonight was the fourth night of revival, and the charged atmosphere was beginning to wear on her. Plus, she was annoyed with Mark's not-so-subtle disapproval of her wearing jeans. When she mentioned, on the drive over, that what she was wearing shouldn't matter, he had said that it *would* matter if she walked down the aisle. When she had assured him that was *not* going to happen, it was as if her words were razors, slashing at him. She had begun to understand that at a church revival there was only one goal: to walk down the aisle or to watch someone else walk down the aisle. With her lack of background in religion Julia wasn't prepared for how offended everyone was by her staying firmly seated in the pew. It was as if her conversion would have been an affirmation of the rightness of their own choices, the rightness of something they had taken for granted since birth. No matter how many times she told Mark she wasn't interested, he insisted that she should give Jesus a chance to speak to her heart, that she shouldn't slam the door without finding out what "He" wanted.

Tonight was Mark's night to testify or she would have tried harder to stay at home. He was walking back and forth in front of the pulpit, down off the risers, on the same level as the congregation, leaving Julia sitting alone in the third row.

"It is only because of the prayers of His saints that I am alive today. About six months after I married my lovely wife, I lay on death's threshold and knew it would be a miracle if I came out alive. I'd like to say that I made peace with Our Lord as I lay there, knowing that my body was failing. But even in that hour, my hardened heart knew not what to do. Instead I lay in my stubborn sin and desperate despair and accepted that death was every mortal man's end, that none of us can fight it. It was only because of the prayers of His faithful that I lived to tell you this tonight."

On the word *faithful* Mark swept his arm, indicating the row of deacons—weathered men, working men, whose wives drug them to the hospital any time a church member was ill to drink coffee out of Styrofoam cups and sit in waiting rooms with heads bowed, forearms on their knees. A few of them straightened up out of that same posture now, uncomfortable at having been pointed out.

"It is only through those who lifted me up with pure hearts, lifted me up on the name of His Son, that I did not perish into the flames of hell forever. I'd like to say that I woke up a changed man, but I woke up a sinner, one not even, as Mary Magdalene, fit to wash Jesus' feet. I spent days recovering and contemplating the helplessness of man, the hopelessness of us all who are dying daily, and not being able to do one single thing about it. Gradually, I realized that Jesus was waiting for me. It is indeed like the song says, 'Softly and tenderly Jesus is calling, calling for you and for me.' I stepped into His arms and I came out of the hospital a changed man."

The organist began to pick out with one soft finger the simple melody of the song. Julia could not sit there any longer, and before she realized how everyone in the room would take it, she stood up. Mark's face went from reverent to celebratory the moment her movement caught his eye. For one panicked second, Julia considered her options, and then she turned and walked along the wall to the back of the sanctuary, through the foyer, and out into the welcome heat of the July night. Before the door closed behind her, she heard the voices of the congregation singing softly, "Come home, come home …."

Julia's story . . . cont.

Mark told me that he couldn't have a child with someone who was an unbeliever. That was the still point for me. Everything soft and tender inside of me turned hard and knowing. I knew that I couldn't stay, couldn't continue our current charade. And of course, things are different now. Something happened—and it wasn't just my leaving—something . . . .

Did it all start with Mark's appendix, or with me inviting Charlie to dinner, or with me choosing to go to Live Oak Camp to be with Charlie, instead of running home to Mandy and Rick? Or did it start with some other catalyst, some other opening? All I know is that when I walked out of that revival meeting, things started happening.

It was a bad night. Bad for Mark. Bad for me. I packed a bag, and the next morning I called Charlie to meet me at 3R headquarters so I could leave my car there. The roads out to Live Oak are rough and that one creek crossing gets worse all the time.

Charlie is like sunshine or perfectly baked bread, all golden and brown. Even when her face and hands are dirty, she looks elegant. Like her body is put together right. Like her joints and muscles are parts of some fluid sculpture. And she is warm like sunshine, too. Her skin is like a heater, and it even makes her hair warm. I could wrap up in Charlie's hair. In the smell of her. And her hands make me want to cry, all blunt-fingered and square. So I went to her . . . and no one was more surprised than I was.

The first week that we were friends, Charlie and I dug and planted my garden, actually a much bigger and more involved garden than I ever intended. It took us three days, with her showing up bright and early each morning full of plans and ideas. Before she drove away that last evening, the job finished, she repeated her watering instructions over and over until I finally had to write them down. I remember scrubbing the black dirt from under my fingernails at the bathroom sink and wishing there was some reason to see her again soon.

I guess she felt the same way because the next afternoon, she showed up at my house with a mess of early strawberries, a cake, and some leftover bedding plants. She wouldn't tell me where we were going and surprised me by bringing me out here to Uncle Bill's. He wasn't here when we first drove up, but she moved around in this house and on this porch as if she owned it. I remember the cottonwood trees had the palest green leaves on them, and the sun was almost hot. Charlie laid out the pound cake and the strawberries, digging through drawers until she found a yellow dish towel to use as a tablecloth, blue tin cups for the lemonade. She made it look like a party, like an artist had laid the table. When Uncle Bill rode up, we were on our knees, digging in his flowerbed, getting dirt under our fingernails again. He leaned on his saddle horn, shaking his head, saying, "Charlie-girl, Charlie-girl."

I had met him months before, and my first impression of Uncle Bill was that of the quintessential cowboy, the real deal, even a sage, though that word isn't exactly right. By then, I was used to seeing cowboys, smelling cowboys, talking to cowboys, but with Uncle Bill, I saw such a perfect icon for the cowboy that at first, I didn't look beyond it, didn't see that he was something more. I had heard Mark talk about him from the beginning, how Uncle Bill was somebody special on the Benson Ranch, how he had run the whole thing for years, but when the board of directors insisted on computers and complicated accounting, he moved over to Cottonwood Camp and ran this part of the ranch almost separate from the whole. Mark always said that Uncle Bill was a wasted resource. Mark trusted and respected him, and I knew that he wished he could spend more time with him. Mark drove out to Cottonwood Camp a couple of times a month, not so much to check up on Uncle Bill, but to sit and talk with him about all that was going on around the rest of the ranch, with the weather, with the employees, with the cow markets.

I had seen Uncle Bill several times since moving out to the ranch, but here was Charlie, acting like she owned the place and grinning up at him as if he were some sort of grandfather. At the time, I thought his face was hard, not really kind, but I came to see him as the kindest man I have ever known. One thing I remember from that afternoon was thinking how much he loved Charlie.

After he unsaddled and washed up, we had a grand party, complete with music and laughter and stories. It is one of those memories where the colors and sounds are all blended up. The gray boards of the porch, Copper lying at our feet never begging, the slanted sunshine, the frail tomato plants that Charlie finished planting while Uncle Bill and I talked. I felt an utter sense of peace, one that wouldn't return for me until much later in the summer when I was back on this same porch. Listening to Uncle Bill was a surprise for me. I didn't expect him to be so well-read, so articulate, so discerning. Hearing him speak of current affairs, of Rilke, and of the weather with equal ease . . . it made an impression on me. It added a zing to the afternoon—like the pound cake. I expected it to be lemon, but instead, Charlie had made it taste like almonds.

That was the first of several parties at Uncle Bill's, and they never got old for me. When we came up out of Slide Canyon, Cottonwood Camp was the only place I wanted to go. And I got my way.

Anna left me. She left me in the wintertime and there never was a winter so dark. We had four precious years together and never did get married. If I could do it all over again, we'd still be living in sin. I promise. We'd be sinning up a storm—two old people just a'sinning and a'loving. I would easily put up with the hard words and the judgmental looks from the community, those things that seemed to mean so much back then. Benson didn't care. He loved Anna, too, and wasn't one to worry about formalities. I thought the gossip was hurting her, but now that I look back on it, maybe the gossip was hurting me. I wanted everyone to love Anna, see her the way I saw her, not as some homeless waif taking a free ride from the Benson Ranch foreman. Even, I guess, I wanted them to think well of me. I was in that middle part of my life when a man cares what people think, is arrogant enough to believe that they really are thinking about him. The beauty of being an old man is that even if they were, and they're not, I wouldn't care anymore. What I do care about is telling the true things I have learned while living this life.

Anna never let on about her past, didn't tell me anything about her family or her growing up years. She's filled in some of it now, in her letters, but back then I didn't push. I wish I had. I wish I had made her tell me the truth. If she had told me that she had run off from a sorry S.O.B. and was scared to file for a divorce because he'd know where she ran to, I would have just loved her and lived with

81

her, protected her the best I could, and never looked back. But she didn't tell me the truth. Instead, she kept saying she didn't believe in marriage. Stubborn little fool that she was matched the stubborn fool that I was.

I can see now that her leaving had to do with other things, too. For over three years, Anna beat out every track I made. Anna got good at doing this work, loved this life, and would have made the best helpmeet a man could have asked for . . . socially, intellectually, spiritually, physically, horseback and in the daily routines of life. But I messed up. When Anna and I finally left the 3R to its new owner, new crew, we moved into the foreman's house at Benson Ranch headquarters. Benson had been making do without a cow boss while I was finishing up to the south, but he was more than ready to turn the running of the crew over to me.

For a handful of years before Anna came, I had worked cows alone. After she came, it was just the two of us, taking it slow and easy, culling the old bitches that ran off and stuck their heads in the bushes time after time. I had stopped using dogs and had watched the cows get gentler and gentler, even in that rough old country. I had skidded some little sheds in to each set of corrals so I could store hay and cubes in them, started feeding a few pounds per head every time the cows got to the pens after we made a drive. There were a lot of things I had learned while working alone that made me a different kind of hand than the wham, jam, rope 'em and choke 'em kind. And Anna had been there beside me most of the way.

We could do just about anything, just the two of us, that needed doing. We branded all of the calves for two whole springs without any additional men. We handled quite a few longears, big ones, when we were getting that ranch clean. I think even now of how quiet some of our drives were, the cows moving single file, right down the trail, the way cows like to move.

But, when I took over the Benson Ranch, I inherited a crew of men. A crew of men who were used to deep tracks and thin shit in front of them, the "all asses and elbows" kind of cow works. All of a sudden, it wasn't just me and Anna, but me and a whole crew, most of them with their ropes readily at hand. Anna got left at home, at headquarters no less. Left to keep house and plant her garden and wait for me to come in. Keep my shirts washed and a meal on the table. I know now that I made a pretty big tactical error. We had let the issue of marriage lie, and she had stopped always looking over her shoulder for the man her old self was tied to. But now I was leaving her, showing her a disrespect that had never been a part of our relationship. I didn't mean any disrespect, didn't mean to take that part of our deal away. But I had an agreement with Benson and it included running his crew as well as a lot of long hours and a lot of responsibility I had not faced before. To say I felt the stress and brought it home with me would be an understatement.

Change is the one thing we can count on, but that change could have been handled differently. There was no reason that I couldn't have included Anna, at least some of the time. I wish I had given her credit. Instead I acted like she should change her whole role in my life. I wasn't very smart back then, and maybe not now, but hindsight shows me a picture I could have painted differently.

I remember one particular day when I told her she couldn't go horseback with us and how she showed up at the corrals mid-morning with one of the other cowboy's wives with coffee and brownies. They left the truck running because the other wife had babies to keep warm. I didn't take time to snack and visit, just gulped down some coffee and got back on my horse to finish sorting yearlings because I had a truck scheduled. When I looked back over my shoulder, there was Anna, the girl I had spent all of my time with for three years, the one person I knew who loved sorting cattle as much as I did. The wind was blowing cold and she had one of my old Carhartt coats wrapped around her. Her hair was whipping around her head, and she was watching every move I made.

That evening, when I came in all give out and wondering why anyone in their right mind would want to cowboy for a living, the house was warm and glowing, the pot of chili on the stove smelled spectacular, and standing in the middle of all of that goodness was Anna. Her hair was curled and she had on some kind of skirt thing. There was pink stuff on her mouth, and there was blue and black glittery stuff around the saddest eyes I have ever seen. I think she was trying to show me that I was putting her into a cage when I took away the work we loved to do together, but also showing me her own willingness to try the new way. It put me on the fight, I guess. Those sad eyes, coupled with my fatigue and my own guilt over something I didn't know how to change were more than I could take. It was the only real fight we ever had, but in a couple of months she was gone, and I let her go. I let her go even after I read her letter of explanation, written on a bank envelope, all messy and mixed up with cross-outs and too-heavy underlining and drawings, sometimes, in place of words. I still have that letter in her wooden chest.

She's forgiven me, you know. She's had a few years of her own to point the way to compassion and understanding and acceptance. All that happened back then has gone down the river. Regrets are useless to carry around, but more than anything I wish Anna and I had children together. We would have had beautiful babies. Smart, too. Even now, when I think of her carrying my child, when I think of putting my seed into that beautiful girl, I feel the heat of our old fire, feel its burn and its pull. I wish we had grown old together.

After all these years, Anna has become what she was at the beginning—my best friend. Rarely a week goes by that I don't get a letter from her, written over the course of several days. I wish I was as faithful to do the same. All those years ago, she sent me a post office box address about three months after she left. In the beginning, I sent letters there, angry ones, begging her to come back to me. I knew that the address was in the town where her sister lived, and her sister was the one who forwarded them on. The first time she answered me back, she was in limbo, up in Montana, working in a hamburger joint and making wind chimes for local tourist shops, scheming on a caretaker position for the winter. The idea of Anna in the world but not in my arms was so painful, and I was working so hard, that we didn't correspond much. Mainly we exchanged brief notes so I knew when she moved to California, went to college, finally got free, met a man who loved her, and had a baby girl. At times, I would let the conversation lapse and there would be long quiet spaces but, after several years, I began getting real letters from her real address. By that time, I had been married to Hope for a decade. It was too late for anything other than what we have, which is a weekly, daily, intimate correspondence, an exchange and a witness of each other's lives, even at a distance. Just a couple of years ago, she lost her husband to cancer. I wonder every day if maybe I ought to drive out to see her. She says she'll come this way someday, too, but I doubt either of us ever does.

We send poems to each other. I know her by her poetry as much as by her letters. Several of them have become the lyrics to songs I play on the fiddle, words I think silently as I play the notes. Silly maybe, for an old man, silly for two old people, maybe, but love doesn't consider wrinkles or years or even distance, now does it? In my mind, Anna looks just like she did back then, filling soda cups at the Dairy Queen, dipping ice cream cones in chocolate.

Not a day goes by that I don't thank the universe for having Anna in it. I send her a flower pressing every spring, send her a sherd of pottery or a perfect point when I find one, send her a dried morel in the fall from down in the creek, from a place I call the "putting green." I need to make sure that when something finally happens to me, someone will call her, will give her little book of poems back to her. I know she has others, many others, but this one is special.

I live with pieces of who she is surrounding me. I drink my coffee from that damned coffee mug. I'll not forget that day. We drove in to buy groceries and supplies and there was an arts and crafts fair going on in the square around the courthouse. Before we went to crossing things off our list, we walked through the booths. Most of it just looked like gewgaws to me, but she squealed with delight all morning.

We ate hot dogs and got mustard on our chins. In the pottery booth, the potter had set up a wheel and was turning out cups and bowls. Anna walked along the shelves of finished pieces and touched that mug with a wondering finger. I bought it for her simply because she seemed to want it, not giddy and playing but seriously considering its handmade beauty. Then she left it behind. I've lived with a little fear that it would get broken, but it has survived to warm my hands every morning. And I have her poems to warm my nights. I still touch her birds' nests, her rocks, her books, the stained white shirt hanging in my closet, those things of her that she left. I listen to the wind chimes she made from old silver spoons. They hang from the eaves of the porch, and their voice blends with the songs I play on the fiddle.

When I pull a pair of socks out of the drawer, I see those blue panties from so long ago. Panties don't hold the charm for me that they used to. An old man finds it hard to sleep and hard to work up interest in some of those other sleep and bed related things.

I remember once stopping in at Hope's house in town for some business or other—or maybe it was a holiday—and offering to give her a divorce so she could find someone new. We hadn't lived together for years. She turned toward me—scorn in her eyes—and laughed.

She called me old man. Told me that we were both well beyond someone new. I remember her words: Do you think that either one of us would want to lie down and cheat now? Do you think I am even looking for a man at this time in my life? And you—you wouldn't know what to do with a woman in your bed anymore, and even if you thought you did, I doubt you could.

She may have been right. Old men's libidos go the way of dreams. When I first wake up, those dreams are powerful and real. Then they slip away, leaving a grasping ache that fades swiftly until the dream matters less than the day ahead. So goes sexual desire. Hope's never understood that I will always be a silly old romantic. Since Anna left me, I've been looking for her—looking inside Hope, around Hope, through Hope, in spite of Hope for Anna to drift back into my life, wishing always that she could be more than words on the page.

When Katy built the fire that evening, she gently lifted the fiddle from its case beside the stove. Her fingers left marks in the thin layer of dust that had gathered on the shining wood. She wiped the now-silent instrument clean before closing it inside its case. She said a small prayer of thanksgiving that she had heard that fiddle sing its songs, that she had witnessed loving hands coaxing forth its sweet sounds. As she lay in the darkness of her second night at Cottonwood Camp, she thought how she should have maybe been lonely. But as Uncle Bill's things came to life around her, through his story, she was less lonely than she'd ever been. She dreamed to the music of the wind chimes. She was eager to rise in the morning to begin again, begin reading again. She was eager to know the rest of his story.

I'm falling in love and it's nothing like the movies.

I'm falling in love with hot coffee mornings and cold whiskey evenings and all the long hours in between.

I'm falling in love with a little bay mare who is just as willing at dusk as she was at dawn.

I'm falling in love with cast iron and merino wool and acorns, with a leftover slice of bacon tucked inside a tortilla at two in the afternoon and we're still six miles from home.

I'm falling in love with that kerosene lantern in the old cabin. You know the one.

With the gila monster and his half smile, with granite cliffs etched with a language even I can learn to speak. The figures point the way.

I'm falling in love with sunset skies and unbidden poems.

With kittens in the hay and eggs in the nest and the weight of a burlap nosebag. The patient horses look like veiled women.

I'm falling in love with branding smoke and an easy sort and the first long trot of the year.

With winter solstice and spring snow and summer monsoon and autumn glow.

I'm falling in love and who needs the movies.

I guess you could say that, for a few years, Uncle Bill was my best friend. Did you know that his favorite dinner was fried eggs and fried potatoes with packaged cream gravy? His second favorite dinner was cornbread and milk. He'd cook up one of those cornbread mixes in a small round skillet and then mash hunks of it down in a glass, pour cold milk over the top, and eat it with a spoon. I have to admit, it's pretty good.

I loved being here with him, loved being at Cottonwood Camp. I loved following him all over this country, my horse right behind his, listening to his stories over and over again, talking about cows and weather and wild animals. Looking at tracks. Discussing life. Getting our shirts wet in the creek when the day got hot. Once we built a fire up on the mesa in November so we could thaw out our hands and feet. Of course, I didn't tell him everything like some friends do, and there were a lot of subjects we never even started talking about. He told me about Anna, though, and he always played a new song for me before anybody else heard it.

I don't know anything about music, but I do know how it makes me feel. Uncle Bill said that is the most important thing about music—the feeling, not the technical stuff or the knowledge of it or even how well it is sung or played. Uncle Bill's music made me feel things, things I can't explain.

After I met Julia, after that night when we went over for dinner, I couldn't explain anything. All I knew was that suddenly I had a friend, a best friend, one I could talk to about anything. We talked about men and sex and babies. We talked about books and movies and art. We talked about horses and rain and about the people who used to walk around in these forests and on these hills long before a bunch of rangers or cowboys or hunters all camo-ed up with fancy sights on their guns. After Julia found her first piece of pottery, she went to town and brought home a stack of books about the tribes and weapons and stuff from this area. She really got into it.

You'd think, with all of her book learning, Julia would make me feel dumb. But she doesn't. It's like, the things she knows something about, I want to know. And the things I know something about, she wants to know.

Those first few weeks, we spent almost every day together, even though we had to drive over to each other's houses or meet in the middle. We went hiking. I showed her my favorite places. We cooked. I taught her some stuff about the kitchen, just like my mama taught me, even though, at the time, I didn't even know I was learning. We went on overnight pack trips, usually when I told Cody Jack I would check his fences and water gaps. We swam in that reservoir over by Benson headquarters. We swam in the creek over at the 3R. We planted my garden and hers. We went to town together and made fun of the people we saw. She gave me books to read and cut my hair. She liked to talk about how some guys think that if they put their mouth on a girl's boob and rub rub rub with their fingers, three times clockwise and three times counter clockwise, that they're really a stud, really pleasing their woman. I never even had that, so I just listened because Julia told all kinds of funny stories like that. With most girls

I feel weird, kinda dumb and left out when they talk about clothes and eye goop and guys and stuff. But not with Julia.

I taught her how to tie in fence stays and how not to be afraid of sleeping outside. I told her about my stash of money and where to find it and how much I had to have before I left Cody Jack. But the problem was, after Julia showed up, I didn't want to leave anymore. Cody Jack started ignoring me, I think mainly because he didn't want to have to explain bruises to someone like Mark. I think my friendship with Julia scared him, but he didn't want to tell me I couldn't be friends with her either. I see now that he was scared of Julia, scared she would take me away from him. And he was right to be scared.

But, what I am trying to say is that with Julia around things were better that spring and summer. For the first time in my life, I was living every day, not just wishing I was living. I should have trusted Julia, though. When she wanted to talk to Mark about hiring me, I should have let her. She tried to give me money and told me that if anything bad ever happened and I couldn't get to her, to go to her mom and dad's house. She calls them Rick and Mandy, and even drew me a little map that I was supposed to put with my secret money. If I had wings, we would have gone there, to Rick and Mandy's, when all of the bad things happened, but there were no vehicles left for us to take that night, just horses, and so I went where I knew to go, the only way I knew to go.

Charlie lay back on the slab of rock beside the swimming hole in the finally warm sun of early summer and asked for her favorite poem once again.

Julia sighed, "But Charlie, don't you want to hear something else . . . something new?"

"No, that's the one I like the most."

Charlie shivered as a breeze blew across her damp skin and thought about how good the water would feel later in the summer when she and Julia would come here again, and then closed her eyes as her new best friend started speaking.

She let the nonsense wash over her, this something new that no one ever told her existed, these made-up words with too many ideas that cleansed her of something mundane that had begun to itch and tear at her soul.

"'Twas brillig and the slithy toves did gyre and gimble in the wabe: all mimsy were the borogoves, and the mome raths outgrabe."

There was a movie once with a pretty lady, I think it was Julie Andrews, who sang about the hills being alive with the sound of music. Well, they are alive this morning, here, a far cry from Austria or wherever she was in the film. I think hills can't help but be alive. I've lived here a long time, but I have yet to start taking them for granted. Many a morning I have sat on a ridge as the sun chased the shadows from the cuts, gullies, and canyons down below me. The light slowly separates the grays from the greys, the clumps of brush from the rocks, and, eventually, shows the white faces of the cattle below, or transforms a pile of boulders into mama cows grazing the opposite hillside.

I am not sure that these young men nowadays know anything about all of that. I don't think they know much about the little surprises that happen when a man is on a horse at the hour when the world is waking up. Like the bull snake that crawls past, sated from a night's hunting, and disappears down a hole you never would see otherwise. He always drags his tail in after him. Or maybe a little ground squirrel will crawl up on the boulder right in front of you and give himself a thorough bath, doing the job on his hindquarters with an acrobatic move you'd never think a mammal with a spine could do. Or maybe a hummingbird will come and drink from the yucca or manzanita blooms, and he'll be so loud and so obvious that you wonder why you don't see hummingbirds all of the time. Or maybe a badger will lumber along and dig up one last root before he goes into his burrow to sleep, deigning to hiss over his shoulder at nothing but his own grouchy fatigue as he heads to bed. Or maybe you will ride up on a den of coyote pups playing in the sand and be aware enough to stop and hold perfectly still.

Once, as I rode past a boulder pile I had ridden past a hundred times, looking for holes or down wires along the fence, I glanced up to see a huge mountain lion, a tom, lying on a ledge, his tail twitching as he watched me go by—like I was his own personal parade. That's what some of these boys don't get, these boys who think that punching cows is about the biggest wreck, about making sure your horse is sweaty when you come in on the drive, about making a hand with a rope where everyone can see. The truth is that cowboying is about having brains more than brawn, about stewardship more than a paycheck, about handling cattle more than catching them, about kindness more than macho.

Ah hell. Who am I kidding? I didn't know all of this when I was their age either. I didn't know it was about waking up, loving what the day held. I was doing a job just like the rest of America. Only, my job gave me this country, gave me this office with brilliant lighting. Nowadays I don't live here because of the pay or because there is nowhere else to go. I live here because on mornings like this, the hills come alive for me.

Charlie's story . . . cont.

I was pretty young when my dad got killed, and Uncle Bill was good to my mama. Everyone was, I guess. All Mama did after Daddy died was work. She worked every single day. She cleaned houses to pay the bills, and she cleaned our house, too. She cooked for other people and she cooked a lot for us, too. When I got older and learned to drive Daddy's old truck, I started going to Uncle Bill's and she just let me run off there. I was riding outside horses some, riding fences for local ranches, mainly because people thought a lot of my dad and wanted to help us out. I wanted to learn to pack mules more than anything, not only because they all said my daddy was a good packer, but because I heard a lot of the pack stations in Wyoming and California were hiring girls. That's always sounded good to me, and I think I am ready to try it now— maybe this summer.

When things got bad with Cody Jack, I didn't even think of going to Mama. For one thing, Mama always said that relationships were work, that nothing was perfect. For another, Mama had enough problems and worries of her own to deal with. She and I had fought pretty bad when I went off to the 3R, and fought again when I sorta got married. But the hard part was that Mama would have said, "I told you so." Mama wanted me to go to college. Mama wanted me to act like a girl. I think I missed out on some girl genes. My sister was all interested in hair and clothes and who said what about who, but I was more interested in the tracks Uncle Bill was seeing in the sand down by the creek and the things he could teach me about mules and horses and cows. I think I tried harder to please Uncle Bill than I have ever tried to please anyone else in my life, especially Mama.

I met Cody Jack when the foreman of the 3R hired me to halter break all of their weanlings. Cody Jack lived in the bunkhouse, and he courted me some, I guess you could say. After we had been doing that sort of courting thing for awhile, the cowboy who was living at Live Oak gave notice and Cody Jack and I talked about how cool it would be to get that camp.

We went away to Las Vegas for a weekend and somehow forgot to get married while we were there. Cody Jack drank and watched the girls shimmy around and played cards, kinda boring after awhile. Someone had told me that Vegas was all about selling sex, so I figured I'd walk around and see it since I probably wouldn't ever have that chance again. I wandered around under the bright lights with all of those cars swishing by and through the clatter and clanging of the casinos, closed up in rooms where it is always night. I ate a really bad fish sandwich in a place where the waiters yelled rude things to each other, tried the raw oysters in another place at three a.m. when I thought everyone was usually asleep. I sat and watched some other people eat theirs so I would know what to do. They were ok, but kinda slimy. Some salesman caught me walking by and used this straightening iron on my hair because I didn't know how to tell him no, and then he got all rude when I told him no way did I have two hundred dollars to buy one of them. I put twenty dollars worth of quarters in a slot machine but when I won fifty, I had to get some lady to show me how to take the slip to the window and get my money. And I didn't know how to order drinks there, so I just had a beer. Cody Jack didn't hardly sleep at all, and part of the time I didn't even know where he was. But oh, well. I had to see what it was like in case I never got to go again. When we got back to the ranch, we pretended we had got married so he could get that camp, and he forgot, sometimes, that I wasn't really his wife.

I cared about Cody Jack, even felt sorry for him in a way. I liked being a couple with him at first because he had been to some other places and talked about a lot of interesting stuff. I thought he was a really good hand, thought he knew a lot and could teach me a lot. To be honest, I thought I could help him, too. But I couldn't compete with the dope, with the alcohol, with the stories he and his friends told. I wanted too much from him, I think. I wanted him to be real. And he wanted to be real, too. I know that. When we were both still at headquarters, I listened for hours as he dreamed of nothing more than a camp job on a big outfit. I wish we could have made that come true. It almost did—but the meth and the meanness took it all away.

I wanted to live at Live Oak Camp as bad as I'd ever wanted anything in my life. It is a long ways from anywhere, out there tucked into the bottom of the mountains in a big ol' pile of granite, all surprises in the spring and hawk cries in the fall. I had a garden and my animals, a nice round pen, trails all over the place to hike on, two big Indian houses within walking distance where I found arrowheads and pottery, and once, a perfect awl made out of red flint. More than anything, I wanted to find a turquoise bead. I still haven't found one, but it's funny how what you want with all your heart can change. I didn't get my fill of living at Live Oak—but after Julia and I ran off, all I wanted was to stay in Slide Canyon. And then, when things didn't turn out like I wanted them to, I hurt like I didn't know I could hurt. Now I don't know what I want except maybe to get away from here now that Bill is gone.

Fall isn't coming on—fall has fully come and even almost gone, and while an old man like me is used to time passing quickly, this year it caught me off guard. It doesn't seem like it was only this spring that Julia and Charlie showed up with tomato, cucumber, and pepper plants. I played the fiddle for them while they dug in my weedy flowerbeds and set the vegetables down into the dirt. I don't even know why they did it. They said they had extra plants, and I believed them. It's just the kind of thing Charlie does.

The cucumbers didn't last long, but I enjoyed them while they did, lots of salt and pepper with a little splash of vinegar. The peppers made until the leaves became edged with black from the frost. I gave most of them away because jalapeños give me heartburn and don't set well on my stomach. The last tomato I ate was stunted by the cold nights, a much deeper red than mid-summer tomatoes. The memory of Julia and Charlie, kneeling side by side like two little girls playing in the dirt planting vegetables for an old man, gets all mixed up with my memories of Anna for some reason. Anna always had flowers and vegetables that ran amuck, never fenced in, never in neat rows, just planted any ol' where. She started seeds in the windowsills, sticking the seedlings into the ground wherever she felt like it. I never saw her buy fertilizer or fancy anything. She just enjoyed the plants, pinched on them, guided them up off the ground so that they wouldn't get stepped on, ate things right off the vine with juice dripping down her chin. *Hope had a garden every year at headquarters, neat rows of stingy, stringy plants that drooped if she missed watering them by an hour, sucked up Miracle Grow, and gave off scrawny scarred produce that we ate with lots of salt to make up for flavor.*

Katy's new day had started exactly like the one just past, and it seemed that it would end in a similar fashion if she kept on as she was. No bubble of bored or restless had risen in her yet. She rose and pulled her camera from its case, weighing it in her hands. Two hours later, she had committed Uncle Bill's home to the camera's memory and her own. Then she went back to her story. His story. The story.

Anna left me lonely.

The cook at headquarters was an old black man named Revis who muttered to himself and kept to himself, puttering around barefoot in his garden when he wasn't scrubbing everything in the kitchen. I think that he missed Anna almost as much as I did. When she and I moved over to headquarters after my job on the 3R was done, she made immediate friends with Revis. She's the only person I ever knew who did, actually. She was often in his kitchen or garden, and he was always giving her stuff or teaching her to cook something. I had forgotten about that until now. About five days after she left, ol' Revis shuffled into my office and asked me if that girl was ever coming back. When I said no, I do believe his cooking went downhill.

I was working almost every daylight hour and some of the dark ones. My whole world was work. My only friends were the men I worked with. The bunkhouse was full of boys who lived for the next big drunk party, the next big wreck out in the pasture, the next pretty girl to make eyes their way. I was certainly past that stage, and I was their boss to boot. My best friend was Benson, but he was also my boss.

I guess everyone thought I needed to get out and be more social, so the women at the ranch badgered me into going to the community pot luck things and the barn dances. I am sure I did not go gracefully. Hope walked over to me at a Memorial Day picnic at the fairgrounds, presumably to rescue me from her son, a gawky pre-teen all gussied up in town clothes, with no spark allowed in his eyes. Hope's husband had left her and those kids, so they needed me. And it seemed as if the Benson Ranch foreman ought to have a wife. Our friends and neighbors must have agreed because they kept throwing us together.

Hope was one of those women who looked so promising, all curves and hair and sparkles, all shiny lips and helpless blue eyes and breathless little voice. She smelled like a department store and made a man want to buy flowers, even though he knew he would regret it once he stepped through the door into the damp florist shop. I never thought about if she had read a book or what kind of housekeeper she was, never thought about how long it took in the bathroom for her to look the way she did, never considered what that stuff on her mouth tasted like. I never thought to wonder if she had ever ridden a horse, or even wanted to.

I've read of people who swept into someone's life. I'd say I picked Sally out of the available lineup, more for convenience than anything else. Anna grew into my life like a plant, something organic and natural, just dawned into my life, beyond my control, something untouchable, unholdable, a meteor streaking across the dark like the ones I've seen when sleeping out on the mesa, up close to the sky. I think I knew from the beginning that Anna was never going to stay. Hope . . . well, Hope "swept" into my life like a clipper ship or a blue norther. I could see her coming but it didn't feel like there was anything I could do about it.

I should have been more aware—should have seen how it would be. The first time she came out to the ranch she wore insubstantial shoes that filled with dirt and horse manure when I tried to take her on a tour down to the barn. Her hat blew off and her hair got all fuzzy looking, and a broken nail ended up being the focus of her afternoon. Reality set in when I finally slept with her and she lay there, all gooey lips and closed eyes and not a sound in the room besides me. Reality set in when she yelled at her kids, lost my place in my book beside my chair when she dusted, screamed when a lizard came into the kitchen, threw away a whole stack of my magazines, and cluttered up the bathroom with pots and creams and elastic stretchy things. Hope had then and has now specific ways she wants things done, a specific agenda for her life. I didn't ever fit into her plans too well, but that didn't keep her from trying to get me to. And us getting married purely fit her idea of what was handy and right.

Sounds petty and childish when I look at it spelled out on the page like this. We all do the best we can, and I'm no treasure. Hope sure let me know that. I work too much, don't take enough vacations. I forget Valentine's Day and check first calf heifers on Christmas Day.

I guess love, the kind of love that the songs are written about, is all that makes living with any one of us worth two cents.

I am still married to Hope. I raised her kids, you know. Never had any of my own, something I regret now. They never called me dad, but they're as close to having kids as I'll ever come. I think being a parent changes a man, makes him less selfish. Helping raise those kids changed me. I owe that part of my life to Hope.

We had a lot of years together, some good, some bad, most of mine filled up with the ranch, especially after Benson got sick. Every day I dove into that dark dank bedroom where he spent the final months of his life. I stood there looking at the shell of who he used to be, holding my breath against the old man smell, listening to him ramble from whatever segment of the past he was living in. I pretended to the world that I was filling him in on ranch business and taking his counsel, but he wasn't able to hear me or help much. Those were the years when his confusion and my stubbornness were collusion, a construct, one I had promised him. I was pretty much on my own.

I worked daylight to dark, and many times before and many times past.

When he died, I tucked the nest egg he left me away in the bank without telling Hope about it, filed the copy of the letter he left me with an attorney, and weathered the months of transition continuing to do what I had been doing for years until the board of directors asked me to be their "general manager." Though I wasn't sure what all a general manager did, I took the title for a few years until it began to set my teeth on edge. But after, I don't know, a decade I guess . . . I felt like I had done my time at headquarters, had done as much "managing" of other men as I wanted to do. I had watched my best friend dry up and blow away, out of life and into whatever is out there beyond it. I tried to do him proud, as if he were watching me from the grave, and though I didn't feel old, I knew I was getting old. I missed living on a cow camp, just tending my country, my animals, having that little bit of freedom that comes with working for wages. As GM, every year I flew to Chicago to present reports to the board, and as I packed my bags that final year, I pulled out that letter of Benson's and added it to the pile of presentations. I cashed in on his promise of a lifetime camp on this outfit. They asked me to continue running the wagon each year, spring and fall, as I had always done, and I obliged them for several more years. Seemed like a fair compromise.

When I moved out here—to Cottonwood Camp—Hope didn't come with me. She had enjoyed being the wife of the general manager, but the demotion to camp man's wife didn't appeal to her at all. She moved to town, and there she's stubbornly stayed. I guess I should be more charitable. After that first time, when I told her of my decision and invited her to come along, I haven't invited her again. She never was much into the ranch deal, always had a teaching job in town and then later became the high school counselor. For her, the ranch was headquarters, and she never saw beyond the drive out and back each day, never knew the names of the horses in my string. She's never been here to Cottonwood Camp.

I drop by her house at some point during the holidays, make sure and check in with her when I go to town so I can tend to any honey-dos. She lives in a house her father gave her when he died, and it's getting all leaky around the seams. But, for the most part, our lives suit us.

I like it here. I re-nailed the roof on that little red barn the other day, where the wind was picking up the tin every now and again. Charlie calls the sound of the windmill "friendly" as it squeaks its way around. I sit on the porch in the evenings and play the fiddle. This house is small, but just right for one old man and his dog.

For years now, I have had Anna, at least in letters. For a long time, they didn't come to my ranch address, the mail that everyone sees, sorted into cubby holes in the office. Anna's letters came to a post office box in town and maybe that was dishonest. When I lived with Hope, the traffic wouldn't bear letters from an old scandal, an old lover. I always told myself that I would tell her if she asked or discovered the truth, but the fact is, I made sure she didn't. It was selfish of me. A few years ago I let go of the subterfuge and closed the P.O. box, letting Anna's letters come straight out here to the ranch. I am too old to hide who and what I love.

Julia's story . . . cont.

For several weeks in there, it felt like every move I made was wrong, every word I said was wrong. Like I was mired in some sort of black mud that held me tight and slimy. I was certain my marriage to Mark was over, and that made me sad, but it was also that my dreams of motherhood and security were slipping away. Plus, I had just found Charlie, this precious treasure who lit up my world and was making ranch life fun. Bearable. It hurt me so much to think about Mark that I just didn't. Hanging out with Charlie was like pain reliever, a throwback to when summer was carefree and all unpleasantness was relegated to the school year. I should have stopped Charlie from loving me so much.

Of course it's easy to look back and see all the ways I messed up. Charlie and I were having so much fun that sometimes I forgot about having to go home to Mark at night and deal with things in a grown up fashion. Charlie taught me about horses and working and how to camp out and breathe without worrying about dirt, weather, pleasing anyone, goals, the clock. I know now that Mark could have shown me those things, would have loved to have been the one . . . but I couldn't see that at the time.

I didn't fit in at the ranch. But you know, at that point I hadn't really tried. I thought, "Oh, well, I am always going to be the boss's wife anyway." I made up my mind that these women weren't ever going to let me forget that I was an outsider. If I had been ranch-raised, or maybe if I had been more eager to dive in and learn about their way of life, I might have met with more warmth. It is definitely partly my fault.

I've thought a lot about what kind of woman chooses this lifestyle. Girls who want to live in the country, away from the pavement, and will put up with all sorts of hardship to do so. Girls who actually fall for the individual under the hat, and don't care where they have to live to be with him. Girls who fall for a cowboy and think that with time, and her guidance, he'll be something else. Girls who want to be cowboys themselves. Smart girls. Dumb girls. Girls for whom the lifestyle is too much, not enough, or simply the life they have resigned themselves to because it is where they find themselves. It's like yesterday they went to a country dance with lip gloss and curled hair and tight jeans, giggling with their friends, and today find themselves pregnant and attached and can't go back to who they were before.

It was my fault that I didn't make many friends, really. But, I had this idea that I would get my thesis written, that I had a real job to do in writing it, so I shut those women out and stared at my computer screen. Played a lot of Bejeweled, to be completely honest, plinking little glowing jewels around on the screen. I wasn't ready to have babies, and most of the women on these ranches have them early on. I didn't drive the school bus or work at the post office in town, plant a big garden and can all of the produce, bake bread, sell Home Interiors or Mary Kay. I didn't even try to go with the cowboys after the first few times I went with Mark.

I realize now that it isn't about belonging or fitting in. It is about making a unique spot for one's self. It is about figuring out how to create a life that brings joy and peace, about producing something of value. I guess Rick and Mandy have known this all along but I am just now catching on. It is about learning new things with an open mind and heart, really listening when someone talks, really listening to what is important to them. Mark does that, you know . . . he listens. He really does love people and tries to understand them and where they are coming from.

That is the part I regret. Mark tried harder than I did. I am trying to make up for that now.

One weekend before we got married, Mark took me horseback. I thought we were going out to his friend's ranch, as in, *his friend owned a ranch*. But actually, we went out to his friend's camp, just one little part of a big ranch, where his friend worked, where he lived on his job.

We drove for miles out of town, and for the first time in my life, I looked at the land. Mark pointed things out along the way, like the cattle, the fences, and the windmills. How much grass was in the bar ditch compared to what was growing inside the pasture. How had I gone all of my life without seeing those things? How had I only seen the ribbon of highway, the oncoming cars, the sky, the mileage signs? Truly seeing the country around us made me feel small. All of my life, I never realized that there was a whole world out there, off the pavement. When we got to the camp, I was impressed with the idea that this friend of Mark's owned a ranch and I made about four stupid comments along those lines before Mark corrected me. "Joel is just a fucking cowpuncher," he said, and I looked quickly at Joel to see him grinning at the shared joke. That was back when Mark cussed.

While we were there, Mark and I rode for what seemed like hours and hours, miles and miles, but turned out only to be a couple of hours and a few miles. I woke up the next morning

Amy Hale Auker

more sore than I have ever been in my life. Mark assured me that those muscles would get used to the new position if I rode enough. So, when we moved out to the ranch after the wedding, I was determined to give those muscles a chance. One day I went with him to ride some fence and put some water gaps back in. One of the things that struck me was how complicated it was to "go riding." I didn't have the right boots and I had to borrow a hat from Mark. Then there were questions about what mount, what saddle, what spurs, length of stirrups, some kind of chaps . . . all of these details! When I pointed this out to Charlie, she said that if she were to go to the city and try to navigate around, it would seem complicated to her, too. She said give myself time to learn it all. Sometimes that girl is so wise ....

That time we really did ride for hours and hours and miles and miles. I was very sore the next day, but the thing that made me not want to go again was that I was bored. Now I look back and realize that I was bored because I did not know how to see. Really see. I never saw the cactus blooms, the berries on the bushes, the birds, the marbled rocks, the lizards. I was just along for the ride, so to speak. Charlie was the one who woke me up. Charlie was the one who taught me to see.

Charlie's story . . . cont.

I've been reading lately, some of those books that Uncle Bill left me. That was something he and Julia had in common, but he left most of them to me, didn't he? There are so many things I wish I could ask him now. I thought I'd have him forever.

I knew he would find us in Slide Canyon. I made us the best little camp. I used the overhang close to the seep that Bill and I had named Earth Mother Spring the time we were looking for remnants and found that one mama cow with like five yearlings following her, all of them sucking from time to time, probably because she had lost her own calf that year. We had the hardest time getting her up out of there. She was a sneaky bitch, ducking into the brush and lying down several times. Those dumb bawling yearlings kept giving her away though. Uncle Bill said we needed to ship her before she taught those young 'uns to do the disappearing act, too. Anyway, I liked that spot, so that is where I took us after the whole ugly thing happened. I drug up enough wood to keep us warm for a whole winter almost, made us a place to sleep with my bedroll laid out on top of all the saddle blankets and pads, fixed our food where I could hoist it up into that grand old cottonwood in a pannier. I found an old log for us to sit on and even made a broom to sweep the ground. I got all domestic. Felt like there was someone to be domestic for.

Julia had a big cut on her forehead, and a pretty nice lump that turned a bright shade of purple. It scared me, but she says now that I exaggerated the whole thing. My cuts and stuff were pretty normal though my back hurt a lot, but I had to use a butterfly bandage to hold the edges of her cut together. Have you seen the scar? I knew it was deep enough to scar ....

Maybe it was the horror of what happened and the fear that Cody Jack might find us again. I would have killed him if he had, you know, to protect Julia. Maybe it was her own story and my story all mixed up together that made us bruised on the inside, which is sometimes worse than a cut that heals. Yeah, I think about it a lot. I would have killed him.

Mark isn't a bad guy. In fact, he is a good guy, a good person. He's just serious and he works hard. And he's pretty religious. Julia is like glitter and fireworks and whipped cream. Mark is like oatmeal and math and taking vitamins in the morning. I told this to Bill one night on the porch this summer, after Julia went to bed, and he looked at me, the way he does, or did, right in my eyes, and said, "Well, if we are going to be poets tonight, you, Charlie-girl, are like earth and wind and fire, with a little rain thrown in to smell good." God, I miss him, Katy. I miss him so much.

Mark didn't do anything wrong. Just loved Julia. But loved the Lord more, I guess. I mean, we all knew he'd had a thing for you, Katy, a long time ago, but I think it was more God that got in his way of loving Julia right. He and Julia started fighting right after he got out of the hospital, and that was awhile before me and Julia met. I think Mark was glad of our friendship at first because it gave Julia something to love about living out here. I think he might have been a little jealous later on, like when she would come ride with me. Once when the Benson cowboys came to the 3R for a branding, Julia came over early in the morning with him. We were working at

Goshen Spring, and I always cooked when they were working there because Debbie had to get the kids to school and to her job in town. When I got the breakfast dishes all done and the dinner good and started, we drove over to the pens to watch the guys brand. We stood, leaning against the boards of the fence, and I put my arm around Julia, and she leaned into me. I liked doing that so I could smell her hair. Between the boards of the corrals, I saw Mark look at us, his face so stern, as if he thought we were wrong or indecent. I know that, later on, some of their fights were about me.

The day she left him, I thought he had hit her or something, but he hadn't. They'd only thrown words at each other. I tried to tell her that wasn't so bad, but, you know, Julia is like a child in some ways. She'd never seen a real fight, one with broken dishes, black eyes, holes in the walls, people threatening things too bad to ever repeat the next morning. She's never seen the jagged edge of a broken beer bottle while she stands with her back in a corner and wonders if this is the night when he is really, truly going to carry out those threats, that maybe he means them when his eyes get all wild. She's never run out into the night, into the darkness because it is so much friendlier than what is inside the house. And I don't ever want her to know about things like that.

For her, those fights with Mark were real. And I know they were real for him. He looked like dog shit when I finally saw him, when he came to Uncle Bill's later on. I saw his lips keep hunting for the exact right word. I saw him turn his back on her when she started talking, like if he couldn't see her, her words wouldn't be real. I saw him lay his head on his arm on the hood of the truck before he drove off, like he was carrying a load of shame with him.

On the day that Julia called me and asked to be picked up at headquarters, Cody Jack was away on some bender. It was the first real bender he had gone on that summer, and I was plenty worried, worried that he would come home, and also worried that if he didn't, he'd get fired this time. I am not sure what I wanted, but I know I was glad that the radio phone was working that day, and glad that Julia called me instead of someone else. And truthfully, maybe I thought that having Julia at Live Oak would protect me when Cody Jack got home.

Mark thought she had gone to her folks so he hunted there first, driving three hours round-trip just to check. He came by Live Oak after that, but Julia met him out at the truck and they talked through the open window, real nice and civilized-like. He drove away without coming in the house, and she said she had "bought us some time." She was so sad, though, said she wanted to make her marriage work. I wanted her to make her marriage work too, because I knew that if she left the Benson Ranch, I would have to leave the 3R. I would have had to leave because I wouldn't have been able to stand being there without her.

Bill faced his homecoming with dread as he topped out on the ridge where he could look at Cottonwood Camp below. The tracks that had come from the direction of the Benson/3R boundary and intersected the trail led straight on down to the barn. He reined up for a moment and studied the saddled horse tied under the shed around back of the saddle house. He couldn't read the brand, but he knew where it had come from. In the darkening light he kept his eye on the barn as he went slowly, carefully, down the hill, growling at the little dog to stay at heel. Beside the barn, he made a big show of dismounting stiffly and tying Jeb to the hitch rail, lowering his hand to unfasten the leather button on his chap pocket. The little dog kept looking at the door to the saddle house, but the old man shook his head and hissed "heel" again.

The pack mule eyed the door suspiciously, and Bill Morgan wrapped his hand around the grip of his pistol.

Before Hope and I got married, she only visited the ranch a few times. On one of those visits she touched the one coffee cup, one plate, one fork, one knife, one bowl in my drain board and said, "That looks so lonely!"

Katy's laptop looked like a spaceship that had landed in Uncle Bill's anachronistic kitchen. She wondered if people who stayed alone for long periods of time got a little crazy as she giggled and looked at the drain board where her own dishes rested.

She was being coy, I think, wanting to let me know how full she could make my life. And she did. Next thing I knew, there were unfamiliar things in the icebox, trinkets on the coffee table, fluffy pillows on the bed, some kind of flowery wallpaper border in the bathroom, and a huge pile of dishes in the drain board. That woman likes to use every dish and utensil in the kitchen to make a meal. I had been missing Anna so much that Hope and all of her busy-ness seemed like the perfect antidote to coming in tired to a dark empty house and all of my "lonely" swimming around.

When Charlie and Julia were here, there was a similar kind of glorious chaos that echoed when they left, and there was that one moment of grief when I stood and looked at the last glass that

Charlie drank out of, upside down in the left-hand side of the sink. It wasn't the loss of Charlie that I felt so strongly, I guess, but the loss of Anna, still and always.

In my mind, Anna is tan, soft, full of youth that shines like a light, unblemished. She is ready and waiting for a tasty life. And, in her letters, her voice is that of a young woman with the lovely patina of life's wisdom to soften all of that clumsy enthusiasm.

Katy paused at the big empty space on the page below these words. The paper was stained with a coffee cup ring, and had faded slightly as if the pad had been set aside and in the sunlight for a period of time. At the bottom of the page, in dull lead was one sentence.

Old men aren't supposed to be in love.

She turned to the page beneath where the writing picked up again, this time with a newly sharpened point.

When I wake each morning, for a few brief moments I am still in my dreams, strong, virile, and ready to take on the toughest greenest colt, the wringiest smartest old cow, the sassiest prettiest girl, the loudest fastest fiddle, and a plate of the biggest spiciest chili rellenos from Hatch, New Mexico.

If I lie without moving, eyes closed, my mind still sunk in what used to be, I can hold on to it for a few moments . . . until my stiff joints and full old man's bladder, my mind wrinkled with years, brings me to the present where I'd best ride some of those old *retirees, ship the mossy horned cow that teaches her calf to run off into the brush, be the grandpa with old bones who escorts pigtailed girls gently around the dance floor, and eat my plain fare, the kind that doesn't burn an old man's stomach.*

Ah, but it's the love that is the hardest to let go of—wanting to touch her skin, taste her laugh, get my hands tangled up in her hair, have her whisper in my ear and know that she sees the real me, the me who isn't obscured with gray and creases and time.

It's the cruelest kind of joke, really, the way the young girls hug me, touch me, ask for my advice, as if inside my heart and my pants I am no longer a man, but an innocuous harmless sexless elder, a lamp burned out and set up on the shelf.

Katy pushed her chair back from the kitchen table and pulled on her coat against the returning chill. She slung her camera on her shoulder and walked out to the barn, not really seeing anything or hearing anything except the story inside her head, the story so full of gaps that she didn't have it all straight yet, the story that seemed to have taken over her life and was going to live with her for a long time to come. She knew she had to seek out other voices, hear them tell their own parts, their own stories. She felt heavy with responsibility and after so long being free from tending to anyone but herself, it felt uncomfortable, like a pack when you first lift it and those initial steps on the trail of a long hike. She'd settle into it.

An old mule and a small bay horse poked their heads over the corral fence as Katy approached the barn lot. The sight of them quickened her steps. She scooped out grain and murmured apologies to the animals as if a few seconds and a helping of contrition were going to make up for missed meals. She ducked into the shed to pour the grain into the feed bunks, and breathed a sigh of relief when she saw the big round bale of hay inside its cage and the open gate leading into the horse pasture. So, Mark had tended to that as well. As if thinking his name had conjured him into her evening, she heard a truck rattle over the cattle guard as she was closing the barn door. The Benson Ranch general manager parked in front of the house, but swung his steps around toward the barn as soon as he saw her.

"Don't get mad. I just came to check on you."

"I'm not mad. I was actually thinking about you. I've been closeted in the house since I got here, close to the fire, and I just now thought about the horses."

"Oh, well. Don't worry about them. I put out a round bale and there is plenty of feed in the pasture. Besides, if you get concerned about something around here, you can hike right up there." He indicated a ridge to the east. "I think your phone will hit a tower if you cross your eyes and say some Hail Marys. Might find an arrowhead, too, if you aren't in a hurry." Mark leaned on the top rail of the corrals and looked under the shed to where Budroe and Jeb were enjoying their bonus of grain. "Still got plenty of hay. I'll bring another bale over in a few days." He glanced her way. "Will you still be here? The weatherman says it's gonna warm up."

Katy kept her eyes on the horizon where the sun was beginning to rest on the top of the mesa. "Yeah. I think I will." She turned his way. "How inconvenient would it be for you if I stayed on out here, lived here, for the next few months?"

"Not inconvenient at all. Handy, really. I wouldn't have to come over and check on things as often. These two would be in good hands. I'm not going to fill this camp anytime soon, though I will eventually. It's your ranch, you know, Katy."

"No. I mean, I know. But, that isn't the point. I want to stay here, but I don't want to interfere with the running of the outfit. I'm asking because I think this is where I need to be right now. I can't explain it. Kinda crazy, I know."

"Then stay. Stay all summer, stay all year. If I have trouble getting this country looked after or worked from head-quarters, we'll do something different. But stay, Katy." Mark cleared his throat and shifted his weight and tried to put playful in his voice. "What'd he do? Leave you a map to his hidden treasure?"

Katy grinned and looked away. "Almost. Great sunset."

The silence didn't last for the whole colorful show, but it lasted for most of it. Katy thought about that summer when she and Mark had spent so much time together. She didn't feel like the same person, and Mark seemed so much more serious, less given to being dramatic. Almost as if he had been sanded over and lost his glow. Maybe it was just age and she'd have to get used to it. She didn't remember him being so fidgety. He was picking at the fence rail with his fingernail.

"So, how is God these days?"

"Katy." He turned away as if to leave, his voice tired and grouchy all of a sudden, even a little hurt.

She reached for his arm. "Hey. I'm sorry. Really. I'll be nice. What I meant to say is how is Mark?"

Mark propped a boot up on the rail and looked off down the creek. "Oh, hanging in there." He cleared his throat again, seemed about to ask something and then shifted gears. "You met my wife at the funeral. We've had some trouble, but we are working it out. I guess we have to, don't we …" It wasn't a question and his voice was rough and real. "And we are all going to miss Bill." His voice got softer. "He was my friend, you know."

"I know." Katy wasn't comfortable with sharing, but tonight it felt right to share this love, this loss, with someone.

The sun was almost gone now, and Budroe had moved away from the grain bunk to the water trough, swishing his nose through water.

"Hey, I was wondering whatever became of Cody Jack?"

Mark abruptly stopped leaning and stood up straight. "I don't know. Nobody knows." Then he breathed deeply and forced a chuckle. "I think the 3R was happy to be rid of him! They didn't even file vandalism charges for the slashed tires on the ranch truck. Some skuzzy-looking friend of his came around at one point, asking about him, saying that he had hauled him out to Live Oak Camp a few days after the girls went missing. You know he was a tweaker, right? I don't think anyone is taking his missing status very seriously. I'm sure he's long gone by now, off to tweaker land. Ha ha . . . ." The chuckle on the end of the speech strained through the evening.

Long after the dust settled behind Mark's truck, Katy stood in the chilly dusk looking westward toward Eagle Peak. Finally, she shivered and went inside. She'd hike tomorrow, and she might take her phone to check messages. Then again, she might not.

I get drunk on the smell of the dark places in the creek.

I get drunk on the idea that . . . well, on ideas.

I get drunk on frog song and lupine blue and sego lilies and horse sweat.

I get drunk on any moon . . . on the sound of a solitary quail at dawn, on the white foam around a baby calf's lips and the lowing of his mother when he strays too far.

I get drunk at five a.m. when I wake to see Orion directly overhead.

I get drunk on long, hot hour-slog days and cooking out of doors.

I stagger.

Forty miles from the nearest Pizza Hut, Charlie made a big mess of fried potatoes, and the girls sat in a pool of light in the kitchen of Live Oak Camp, dark windows all around, eating the hot potatoes with cold ketchup and too much salt, right out of the pan, licking their fingers, elbows on the table.

Julia grabbed an old envelope and began making a list of "girl food" to be bought in town the next day with Charlie grinning awkwardly at what surely had to be a fantasy list, given the level of her bank account. She was excited by the implication that Julia was going to stay awhile, long enough to eat all of those things, some of which Charlie had never tasted.

"Shrimp, sushi, of course with pickled ginger. I have to have ginger with my sushi. Chocolate chip cookie dough ice cream, pretzels, crab dip . . . do you like crab?" Julia looked up at Charlie, pencil poised above the paper, her face serenely serious.

"Grapes. Red or green? Dr. Pepper, olives, brie. Oh, and some good crackers. Avocados, a good merlot, and maybe some Captain Crunch for midnight crises . . . and oh, do you have any cocktail sauce or should I add it?"

Charlie stood up and put the dirty skillet in the sink, absolutely sure that she did not have any cocktail sauce. Her throat was tight. Julia's happy in spite of sad, Julia's enthusiasm rather than inertia—all of it—being here with her—made Charlie positive that if she spoke now, she'd burst into tears.

Charlie's story . . . cont.

Julia started crying first. And she was good at it. She sure knows how to cry. I always have the hardest time crying even when I want to. Julia cried about how could she have married Mark, and what was she doing way out in bumfuck when she had a perfectly good college education and now, no career and no idea how to start one and no babies and no thesis. The last word was the best wail yet. Her tears certainly drove mine away, and I stood there not knowing what to say. I didn't know a thing about a thesis, still don't, and I wanted to say that it was a good thing about the babies if her marriage was falling apart, but I didn't. I tried to say something about it being a long way to town for a career, but somehow that only made her cry harder while she tried to say something about how Mark had said he was watering and tending her garden while she was away. She wasn't making much sense so I did the only thing I could think of. I just wrapped her in my arms until she quit wailing, led her into the bathroom and helped her out of her clothes while the water ran in the tub. I pulled all of that red hair up on top of her head and soaked her in hot water. I don't know. Maybe that was the wrong thing to do, but it usually works for me. Then, as if *she* were a baby, I dried her off, put a big old soft nightgown of mine over her head and led her to the bed. I lay down beside her and wrapped her up in my arms again. That's where we were when Cody Jack found us. He stumbled in, drunk and high out of his skull. He took one look, decided what he saw, and all hell broke loose.

124

Julia's story . . . cont.

When Uncle Bill rode into camp with Charlie, I knew that we'd soon have to make a decision about what to do. It had been so nice down there in Slide Canyon. I had forgotten about long, uninterrupted peace, if I had ever known about it. I think I knew it as a child, lying on my back in my tree house. No books, no radio, no friends, no toys . . . just a long, long hot summer afternoon, nothing to do but lie there and be still. The rest of my life was school and play dates and family vacations and then school and band practice and speech meets and school and dates on the weekends, school and papers to write, summers working at things I wanted to do. I am sure there were days spent at the lake or afternoons reading on my bed or Sunday mornings with pancakes and coffee, but that time down there in the canyon with Charlie was something special. All we had were the basics. Charlie's bedroll, a coffee pot, two tin cups, two tin plates, two forks, a knife. Packages of instant oatmeal, a can of coffee, a handful of teabags, bacon, bread, cans of soup and chili, crackers, and, you won't believe this, a jar of artichoke hearts. Charlie can't remember buying them or even having seen them before. Neither one of us can remember packing them. But there they were in the pouches . . . what are they called? Panniers? Anyway, we ate them with much ceremony, one at every meal for each of us. I saw Charlie wash out that jar and stuff it into her duffle bag when we were at Uncle Bill's, but I didn't let on that I saw. I know that she listens to that old Jewel CD I gave her every night, too. Like all of us, Charlie needs to make her own peace with what happened, needs to figure out for herself how things really are, and if keeping that silly jar helps her, then she should.

We all do what we have to do to make sense of things. See this arrowhead? Charlie found it the first time we went camping together. She gave it to me. Rick has a friend who makes jewelry in his garage, and he made it into a necklace that I wear all the time now.

I'm not a prude. I experimented with other girls in college, and I know that a little bit of intimacy is a big deal. But, for Charlie, it's the only intimacy and sweetness she has ever known. Maybe I made a mistake, but we had just come through a bad time. A really bad time. We both wanted to make everything alright after all of the horrible.

And it was horrible. All of it. I remember crying so hard over hurting Mark, over not being able to be who he needed me to be. I remember taking a bath, and Charlie drying me off, leading me to the bed. I remember being too tired to keep on crying. I crawled under the covers, fell asleep cuddled up with Charlie.

I have nightmares now—when I am right on the edge of sleep, right where that big black hole opens up and you can either go around it to sweet dreams or fall into it where the monsters of the past wait to gobble you up. That is when I struggle the most. That is when I dream of waking up in Charlie and Cody Jack's bed, Charlie hovering over me, protecting me while Cody Jack comes charging in, full of rage, screaming horrible things. It is that rage that waits for me in the bottom of the early sleep dream hole.

I re-live screaming at him to stop while he's punching and kicking Charlie, and then beating her with that awful quirt. The blows sounded just like the word cunt that he kept saying over and over. I wanted to do something and didn't know what to do. I felt helpless, sure, but what is worse is the knowledge that when I picked up that rifle leaning in the corner of the bedroom, it was because I wanted to kill that man, not just make him stop, but kill him.

Only I didn't.

Twice, after we got to Slide Canyon, Charlie went off into a hysterical mixture of wild laughing and crying. It happened once when she was talking about how civilized we tried to be when we first met, before we got to know one another, before we recognized that we have, as my mom would say, known each other all along. Mandy would say it with a lift of one eyebrow, as if past lives are simply a fact, and everyone should just get real and acknowledge them. The other time was that last night in the canyon when we were discussing what happened and she said, "Did Julia SHOOT him? Nooooo! She HIT him with the gun! HIT him! With a gun!" I had to tell her to shut up. I've never operated a gun before. In fact, except in a museum or the one Mark keeps in the saddle house, I don't think I had ever been in the same room with a gun before. I was raised by pacifists, for crying out loud. I think it decidedly unfair for Charlie to make fun of me for not shooting off that gun. How would I have known if it was even loaded or not? What if it had some tiny red button that was a safety or something? What if I shot Charlie instead? Besides, I didn't have time to shoot him. He was hitting Charlie over and over and over and I couldn't take it anymore. I had to stop him. But the scary thing is that I *would* have shot him if I had known how, shot him right in the head, watched his brains splatter and not have cared. That is what makes me wake up shaking and gasping. It scares me to know what I would have done if I had only known how.

It is evening. I have had a long day, a good day, but a long day by any man's standards. The cold wind takes the sap right out of me, no matter how well I slept. I shod a horse this evening. Well, I shod two feet. I'll get the other two another day. The back have to follow the front, is what they say.

Used to, a cowboy only needed to know cows and horses, maybe a little about leather work and rawhide, how to patch up his own gear. He might have needed to know how to open a can, fry a steak, make biscuits, do a little practical vet work, but really, it was mostly about the animals and knowing how to read the weather. Nowadays, a good hand needs to know how to mechanic on a vehicle, re-leather a windmill, set strong brace posts in a fence, maybe do a little plumbing and electrical work, some welding, build a gate, and on some outfits, in some areas, even do some farming. Times have changed and the ranches need their hands to be able to do a lot of different things. It isn't good or bad or even preferable either way. It's just the way things change. I know that when I was running the Benson, I liked hiring a man who was willing to get off his horse and get his hands dirty or greasy. Sure made my life easier.

Speaking of, I went to the old folks home to see Dave Cameron here awhile back. I know they don't call them old folks homes any more. Assisted living. That's where ol' Dave is.

Come-along. That's what we always called him. Come-along. I can't even remember where he got that nickname now, but he was one of the best men I ever hired. About my age. He was purely handy. Could do just about anything, and would. Very good with vehicles and motors. He cowboyed for me for about eight years, lived on the West River Camp, and I never had to worry about him doing his job or taking care of that part of the ranch, he always did more than I asked him to. Had three of the smartest kids I ever knew, and that's why he quit cowboying. Went to running heavy equipment at the mine so he could get those kids through college. And he did, too. All three of them got college degrees, and one of them is working on a PhD. Dave isn't getting around that good, using a cane now. When I drove up, he was out by the garbage can with a little white grocery sack of trash all tied shut, talking to two other old men. While he made me a cup of coffee, he told me that the garbage can is like the old folks' home water cooler. Everyone goes there a couple times of day to catch up on the gossip and tell stories.

Dave always makes me a cup of coffee when I stop by. And it takes him a long time to do it. Each move he makes is deliberate and careful, prolonging both my visit and the task, to fill up his day, I guess. Sad to see a man with such talent watching game shows and old movies on tv.

Every time I visit, Dave tells me his repertoire of cowpunchin' tales. He left the ranches over 30 years ago, and they are all he has. Punching cows is the part of his life he's held onto. And though I have heard those stories so many times I can tell you where the pauses are and all the punch lines, I just let him talk. Doesn't hurt me none.

It seems that no matter what else a man does in his life, if he's ever spent time in the saddle, ever lived the life of a cowboy, those are the days he wants to recall. This time, though, Dave paused about three sentences into his first story and said, "Oh, but you've heard that one before, about the time that brown horse turned over on me in the creek, down in the Basin?" When I nodded, he took a sip of his coffee, and looked down at the scarred table top and laughed without any happy in his voice. "Bill, you son of a bitch, you've heard 'em all, and yet you still let me ramble on." I think the quiet in that room was the saddest I've ever heard. Damn, he was a good hand, a good man.

While I shod that horse today, I thought of how I failed Charlie. Long before she ever hooked up with Cody Jack, I knew what kind of man he was. What I blame myself for is not being forceful enough in trying to talk Charlie out of moving to Live Oak. I wanted, so much, for her to be close, just over the ridge, for her to get to have the life she dreamed of.

I like to think the best of people. I can't remember who said it, but it is true that people will either live up to your expectations or down to them. I think every man deserves a chance to change his reputation at some point in his life. None of us get many chances to do that. I was only ever around Cody Jack a couple of times, in social settings . . . like a barn dance or back behind the chutes at the reunion rodeo. He was cordial to me, deferential even. I wanted to brush the rumors and stories of punchier-than-thou away, attribute them to his being a young man finding his footing in a hard world. But in my heart, I knew better. I'd heard several reports from men whose opinion I respect.

I've been around all kinds, and he was the worst kind. The worst kind of man. He was the kind of man who must take out his frustration, both with himself and circumstances, on something—anything. Usually something weaker and undefended. He was the type who would rather rope and choke a cow than gather her slow and gentle into the corrals. He was the type to pound Copenhagen into her eyes and stomp her with the heel of his boot once he got her roped, thrown, and tied down. The kind who justified his actions by saying that he was teaching the "dumb animal" a lesson while he beat her with a crowbar. He was the kind I would not ever want on my crew or across the fence from me if I owned livestock.

I fed Charlie's dreams of a cow camp, encouraged her, even as I recognized the hard facts. For awhile there, I thought perhaps her woman love would soften a hard hand, a young hand, like Cody Jack. I wish I had just told her to move in here with me. I wish I had been the kind of friend and mentor she needed, but every girl wants love. I wanted that for her, too. Later on, when I knew she wasn't getting what she needed and deserved, I failed her the way I failed Anna. I did not interfere. I was passive rather than aggressive.

I am going to write this part down, but my throat hurts with the memory and I hope no one reads these words until after I am dead. It is hard for me to remember the day, way back last winter, when I was at headquarters and heard a story that chilled me through. Seems as how one of the little gals in town who runs barrels had hired Cody Jack to shoe her mare. It was the vet telling about it so I know it is true. Seems she brought that little mare in to see that vet, get him to help her because the mare was crippled. That vet said that the filly would not even put her right foot on the ground, and she was thin and poor with pain. He said it made him sick to his stomach when he saw, immediately, that there were only two clinches on the inside of the hoof. But when he pulled the shoe, there were three nails, one just as straight as the day it was cast, all the way up inside the hoof wall.

When I heard the vet tell that story, I was scared for Charlie, sure, but I also wanted to kill Cody Jack, not only for the nail, not only for the welts still on that mare's ribs from blows from a rasp, but for the fact that as that gal jumped her out of the trailer, she told the vet that the filly had been like that for two weeks. Said her "horseshoer" told her she'd get better soon. Any man who can leave a creature to suffer, intentionally, that long, is not worth the air he breathes on this planet.

I am old. I know that if a man can have that much of a callous on the part of him that should hurt for others, he's suffered some pretty bad things himself, and instead of learning to care, he just learned not to flinch at making others suffer.

What does that say about me?

"Come out of there."

Bill's words were short and hard, sliced off at the edges. The little dog bared his teeth and his throat quivered, but he didn't leave the old man's side. Cody Jack appeared as a deeper shadow in the door of the saddle house, his pocket knife in one hand, cleaning the nails of the other. He grinned.

"You old bastard. You found them, didn't you? How come they're not with you?"

Bill stayed still and quiet.

"Well, you were smart not to unsaddle. There's more riding to do tonight. Put that gun away, old man."

Cody Jack waved his knife and put his head to the side. Uncle Bill kept his pistol firmly in hand.

"Gun or no gun, you're gonna take me to those girls. I have to teach that bitch that she can't never leave me, especially not for a redheaded dyke."

Cody Jack turned towards the 3R saddle horse tied up under the shed.

Bill had already seen the wild hot eyes. He had already weighed the circumstances, already measured the chemical-altered character of the younger man. He felt the coldest knowledge of his life rise up from his belly and lodge itself in his heart.

When Mark drove over the cattle guard into Cottonwood Camp, he was surprised to see Bill's horse standing between the house and barn, bridle reins dragging. Mark stepped out of the truck in front of the house and walked toward the saddle shed.

The little dog whined from the doorway.

A good story has action in it, and I am not telling a good story. I wasn't there for much of the action. I was there for the healing, for the long lazy days when the cicadas sang back and forth and the water in the creek flowed less and less and the wounds slowly mended. I was there for the stories, for the re-telling, for the tears. I was there to bring those girls up out of that canyon. Here at Cottonwood Camp life sorted itself out, as life often does. I hugged them goodbye when they left, and nothing much has changed. I am alone again. And yet, everything has changed.

Even when it seems as if one day simply flows into the next, as if nothing is ever going to break loose, as if nothing is moving, there is change. Water comes up in the creek, seeds form in the pods, teeth loosen in the young and old, leaves decay, insects go though their never-ending metamorphoses, love blossoms or fades as the season may be. And though my life alone looks the same as it did on the surface, as it did before those girls jumped ship, broke the mold, bucked off the bridle, fled the reservation . . . pick your metaphor . . . it is changed, way down deep underneath the crust.

Katy got the fire going again and spent some time preparing her meal, enjoying the simple processes of baking a potato, making a salad, and forming a hamburger patty from the package in the sink before stowing the rest away in the refrigerator. She set the table and combed her hair. She ran her finger along the rows of books on the shelves but, instead, chose to read from the fragile book of Anna's poems while she ate.

The beat of the heat is a refrain as we strain toward the hope of rain with dust under our feet and the crust of dried-up ponds mocking the month and the dense blue of the rueful rural sky.

We all say the same thing when we gather—palaver, an old-fashioned word that has seen other dry-fry summers—and I wonder as we stand in the hot wind and slow burn which of these be-hatted men also mourn the loss of lust when the sheet is kicked away by impatient feet and even the early morning is another long, slow wait, grate, uneasy fate, gray slate of un-puffed sunrise, then red red red.

There is no poetry in July.

While her dishes dripped in the drain board, she slipped on the oldest and softest sweats she owned, added a night log to her fire, and took the greatly diminished stack of yellow legal tablets to the couch. The soft old quilt felt like a friend.

I checked water gaps today after the rain we had two nights ago. Nothing completely washed out, though I cleared some debris from a couple, spliced some broken wires, cut a few new stays. I saw a Mississippi kite. Felt winter moving in. The puddles of juniper berries that were vibrant blue like something on a children's playground have faded to softer lavender. The leaves that were gold and red are peach and pink now like crumpled tissue paper that has been left out in the rain. The bird nests in the deciduous trees are visible against the sky, no longer hidden from view and private.

A fire feels good tonight. That old Jasper horse didn't come in at chore time. I'll have to saddle up and find him if he doesn't come in tomorrow. Sure hate to see him go, but I'd rather he went in the fall, before it gets too awful cold, than to see him lose flesh the way he did by March last year.

There was another asterisk and this time Uncle Bill's notation in the margin was a date in mid-January and the letters *RIP*.

I wrote many of these same words today, addressed them to Anna before I returned to these pages. A part of me wonders why I am not sending this whole story to her, but somehow I have to choose the right person, someone who knows the cast, someone who knows me but not as well as Anna does. While I won't apologize for what happened, I am also not proud of it.

Whoever said familiarity breeds contempt was wrong. The longer I love Anna, the more I come to know her, the more familiar we become, the less I want her to see my failings. Familiarity only breeds contempt when there is something contemptible. When love acts like a spotlight, it should stir in a human being the desire to be a better person, to be the best he can be.

I have written many pages without getting around to the real story, but one thing I want to say before I go on is that I hope that my love for Anna, my love for Richard Benson, my love for Charlie and Julia, the good things I have done in my life will outweigh the bad, will outweigh the things I am not so proud of. I am no different than any other man, may even have turned into a cliché here at the end, trying to put my house in order, so to speak. One thing I know, there's no point in trying to fight the story. Paper is cheap, and I've read a lot of other men's stories. It's high time to tell my own.

And Katy Benson slept, in a place that felt like home.

Charlie's story . . . cont.

Bad things happened when Cody Jack came home that night. After I got Julia out of the bath, we fell asleep, you know, the way you do after a whole lot of emotion. I had become a light sleeper, always wanted to know where Cody Jack was those days, but for some reason, with Julia in my arms, I fell asleep deep and hard. I woke up when he turned on the hall light and it fell across the bed shining on Julia's bright hair on his pillow, my arm around her waist. I knew immediately what he thought he saw. He was just a shadow in the doorway but I knew it was him. Like I told the sheriff when he came out to Cottonwood, it was all a blur for the next little bit. I had gotten pretty good at defending myself, but I wasn't strong enough to defend Julia, too.

Cody Jack was very strong when he was all hopped up, and he got me down awfully quick after I got between him and Julia because I was tangled in the sheets. He made sure to stomp me with his boot once I was down. What I can't figure out is why he already had that quirt in his hand. He must have grabbed it from where it hung on the wall in the living room but—weird—in all the times he decided I was not a cooperative little wife, he never thought to use that quirt. After the head stomp, all I could do was protect myself. Julia, later, made a big deal out of the marks on my back, but the fact is, they hurt less than knowing she was hurt, less than her witnessing me that helpless.

I didn't realize that Julia hit him with the barrel of the rifle. Cody Jack was yelling horrible things about what he thought was going on between me and Julia, about how he thought Julia was stealing me from him. All I knew is that he stopped with the quirt and turned with one of those enraged sounds I had come to know so well. When I looked up, through the fall of my hair over my face, I saw Julia swing again, and Cody Jack put up his arm to block the blow. Then he caught the barrel of the rifle and flung it back and away. Julia's arm swung up with it and she stumbled, the barrel striking her squarely above the eyebrow. She made a noise that I hear in my sleep, though I don't have the same kind of nightmares she does. The noise was like a child would make, and she reached up a finger to her forehead. I think it was that sound and that innocent gesture that brought Cody Jack out of his kick-your-ass rage. From where I stood, it looked like her finger had turned on a spigot of blood, and it flowed like a river down into her eyes, each indention in her face catching a puddle. He just stood there and stared. Julia lost all other color from her face. It was just red and white, pale enough to make me run over and hold her up.

Cody grabbed my arm and dragged both of us, me holding onto Julia, shoved us into the bathroom, and slammed the door. I locked it. We stayed in there for a long time—even while he came and yelled at me through the closed door, telling me what he was going to do if I ever called the cops on him. Like I could have. I found the pieces of Julia's cell phone on the kitchen floor later, stomped with his boot heel just like my head. The radio phone was ripped from the wall. He yelled all this nonsense, telling us he was gonna come back for me, telling me he would never lose me to some pussy licker or split-tail whore. I am sorry to say it all with his language, Katy, but I am just trying to tell the truth of it.

All I could do was hope the lock held on the door and hold the towel more firmly to Julia's cut. We didn't dare go out of the bathroom until we heard him drive away. When he was good and gone, I took the flashlight and saw that he had left us with no keys for the ranch truck, plus had slashed all four of the tires. He took most of his personal belongings, though he didn't have many left. Things had been disappearing for a long time, sold for drugs I guess. He took my little truck. The cops found it in town, out of gas.

Katy, see, on that night . . . we just needed to get away from there.

Who knew when he would sober up and decide to come back, right? I tried to explain that to Uncle Bill, how I couldn't just sit there, how I wanted to go somewhere safe and breathe. Sometimes I didn't like talking to Uncle Bill, especially when he listened with his eyes on the ground and his lips pursed and he said, "Hmm ...." Made me think he didn't really believe me. I was telling him the truth, but there was also a little bit of me that wanted to leave the world behind, leave the Marks, leave the Cody Jacks, even leave the Uncle Bills who would try to talk sense into us. I wanted to leave the gossip behind, leave behind some of the complicated questions I had begun to wonder about since I met Julia. What's wrong with taking a few days, during nice weather, to sleep outside and hang out with someone you really like? Especially in as beautiful a place as Slide Canyon.

It must have been way past midnight when Cody Jack woke us up because it took until dawn to pack the camping gear, my bedroll, and some food. We patched each other up the best we could, and loaded the mule. I grained all the horses good and, as the sun came up, I turned the remuda out of the corrals, and we rode out right along with them until we got to the north gate of the horse pasture. From there, I didn't even try to hide our tracks. We headed straight for Slide Canyon because I could see that Julia was not going to be able to ride very long. My eye was starting to throb. Once you get over the mesa, the way to get down into the canyon is pretty easy if you know what cow trail to take off the main track. It winds through the thickets and some deep sand, but once you drop down over the edge, it snakes its way through a big boulder pile and then down into the prettiest place I've ever seen. We didn't even bother to set up camp at first . . . just unloaded the mule, unsaddled the horses, staked the livestock, and unrolled the bedroll in the shade. We lay down side by side and let the sun slide over the top of the sky, getting up from time to time so I could drag the canvas bedroll tarp along the path of the shade.

Later, when we were rested, it started to feel like a holiday. We pushed the ugly night away and started having fun. It is hard to explain but breaking up dry wood, building a fire, cooking, eating, fixing a cup of hot tea, watching the sparks fly up—it felt like a party. I knew we couldn't stay that way for always, but I knew that we were going to get to lie down together and sleep through the night. If we were lucky, it might be three or four days before someone came looking for us, and if they didn't, well, eventually we'd go to Cottonwood. I was both right and wrong. It was four days before Uncle Bill showed up, but he gave us that extra night before he escorted us home. Even then, I still got to be with Julia for a few weeks longer at his house.

I won't ever forget those nights from then until Julia went back to Mark. We kept each other warm, whispered to each other at intervals during the night. We soaked in the swimming hole. We ate those damned artichoke hearts, doling them out as if they were magic. At Cottonwood Camp, we slept in Uncle Bill's bed and I listened to Julia sigh beside me, dodged when she flung her arms about in her sleep. I cooked for them both. We read, laughed, sang, told stories. I memorized that Jabberwock poem so I could say it with Julia, and her face lit up when I got it right.

Of course, I knew it had to end sometime. I thought that she was going to go back to town, to her thesis, to her life before the ranch, to her friends, and to a lawyer's office to file divorce papers. It was hard for me because I didn't know if I wanted her to leave Mark or stay with him. I knew that if she left him, I would lose her. If she stayed, maybe Mark would have hired me to ride colts and live at Benson headquarters, and I could have kept her happy. It was confusing because I didn't even have a place to live. Uncle Bill said Cody Jack was long gone and not to ever worry about him again. The sheriff asked me if I could help find him, which made me believe that Cody Jack had no intention of being found. I knew I could live with Uncle Bill. That was clear from the beginning—for a long time, really—offered in Uncle Bill's backhanded way. I mean, it all worked out . . . especially when the foreman of the 3R came out and hired me back to live at headquarters. I think he felt bad about what happened. All I had to do was shift my stuff from Live Oak to the little trailer behind the cook shack. It's kinda shitty that they wouldn't hire me to just stay on at Live Oak. I mean, I had been doing Cody Jack's job for months. I'd been riding his fences, checking his waters, caking his cows, putting his water gaps back up, even climbing the windmill tower to grease the dang thing. But girls don't hold down camps, at least not on big outfits, so I went back to headquarters.

Julia and I had a fight about me going to college. She wanted me to go to classes and Starbucks and write my own thesis. In other words, be like her. And she accused me of wanting her to live like me. I don't understand any of it, you know. What I wanted was for us to be together. What she wanted was for us to be pals. I should be happy for her now, I guess, with the baby coming and all. With her and Mark back together. I should be happy for the three of them.

I am trying.

On our last night in Slide Canyon, after Uncle Bill left, I asked Julia about the future. We were sitting on the log with our dinner plates in our laps. I didn't know how two women went about loving each other. I just wanted to know about the future. Julia and I were always holding hands, and hugging, and we had started kissing each other . . . not like guys and girls kiss, just silly and, well, I don't know how to explain it, and I don't feel like trying. But when I brought up what was going to happen after we left the canyon, I found out that things weren't the same for her as they were for me. At the time, I was angry, but now I realize that maybe I was so sad it felt like angry. I yelled at her, my voice bouncing around the canyon like bullets. I asked her what about the times we slept in each other's arms, what about the times we said "I love you."

Katy, I don't know what you plan on doing with this story, with all of the stories. I guess all I can do is tell mine. This is the point in my story where I got my heart broke. I thought if Julia wouldn't listen to my words, I could show her how I felt. When you love someone, you want to show them that love, right? Not be like buddies or roommates. But Julia, well, she wouldn't let me. She actually pushed . . . pushed me away and then she just sat there, her arms wrapped tight around her waist and cried, "I do love you, Charlie. I love to be all cuddled up with you, but not like I can love a man!" And I realized how stupid I was.

Most of the tracks made that night were by moon shadow.

Mark cleaned and tied up the big gash in the old man's arm the best he could. And while that arm looked bony and thin to the younger man, he knew it contained a strength he could never match. Mark helped load an unholy burden onto the mule, the mule who hadn't taken one step from the hitch rail when the scuffle was going on, had endured even the sound of the gunshot that had spooked the little bay horse, causing him to take several rein-dragging steps and widen his eyes and nostrils.

The mule stood silent and willing under his gruesome load.

They left single file, two men horseback, one leading the mule, the other leading the dead man's horse, still saddled.

By dawn, both men were exhausted. Through the long hours of the night, tracks had been laid in the dirt, between granite boulders. A saddle plus the mule's burden rested at the apex of a peak that was really just a pile of boulders, stacked by an enormous ancient mythological hand. The men paused at the base of the hill, ready to go their separate ways, make separate sets of tracks.

"Thank you. You are a fine young man. I am sorry I have made this mess."

"You didn't make it. Are you okay to go on alone? Are you bleeding through the bandage?" Mark tried to reach for Bill's arm to take a look, but the old cowboy shifted and smiled a tired smile that made him seem older than Mark's new-found God.

"Just a scratch. Go on with you. And check that water gap below Cedar Bench on your way home. I haven't been by there in awhile."

Mark turned to mount up, chuckling. "Look, you lazy old man. I am not going to check water gaps for you. I'm the boss, remember?" As he rode away, he wondered how they could smile and joke at all, or maybe smiling and a few mild jokes made it all bearable.

Bill and the mule and the bay horse and the dog left Eagle Peak, circled around to Slide Canyon once again.

Mark made tracks almost all the way to Live Oak Camp. He stopped at the top of the horse pasture and led the spare horse though the gate. The tracks that went on from there were those of a lone saddle horse going toward the Live Oak barn in the meandering, grazing way of a horse with no rider. That job done, Mark turned and slow jogged to Cottonwood where he turned his weary horse out and took his own weary self home to headquarters, hoping no one had noted his absence through the night or noticed his driving around at an odd time of dense early morning. He thought of the words that William Morgan had spoken to him as they stood high on Eagle Peak.

"It would have been easier for us to have called the law. They would have considered it self-defense, I know. But I thank you for indulging me this sky burial. Do not let this event and your part in it shake you or define you. Right and wrong are colorful things, and they change shape on us. I am not going to preach to you, and certainly not going to preach above this sorry body. Rest easy, my friend. I ask only one other thing of you. Please allow me to die in my own peace, someday, if you would be so kind."

Mark had learned enough about resting in peace that he decided that he would, indeed, let the things that needed to rest be at rest, even in his own soul. But he knew, too, that sometimes in the dark, he would imagine the desperate struggle that must have taken place in that dim saddle house at Cottonwood Camp. The dusty battle with one man so good and one man so bad, one man so young and one man so old, one man so wise and one man so foolish, one man so strong and the other so weak. And he lived his own life so that he knew which kind he, himself, was.

Before Uncle Bill got all the way to Charlie and Julia, who were awake early, packing up camp, he stopped, loosened the cinches on his animals, made a roll from the old coat tied behind his saddle. He lay down beneath a juniper tree to rest before he fetched those girls, fetched those girls home.

I am up earlier than usual this morning, barely morning. I dreamt of Wichita Canyon, way on the south end of the 3R, a place I haven't been in two decades. And yet, that's the thing about the natural world. I don't have to go there to know that it's there, to know that the pink penstemon will clash with the Indian blanket and the desert paintbrush, that the tadpoles will grow legs and hop away or die as black mush in a puddle that turns to mud too early under the hot sun. I don't have to go there to hear the canyon wren in my head, its sweet song the sound of alone but not lonely the way the hawk's cry is. I don't have to go there to know that year after year, hidden away in its deep slots, elk come to drink, skunks live and die, dens and nests fill up with eggs and young, carnivores eat, herbivores graze, sego lilies bloom, water makes noise as it flips itself over rocks even when no one is there to hear. How often have I felt like an intruder as I hunted for cows in those places where the squirrels stayed and looked and asked to be noticed simply because they had never seen a human and probably never would? How many creatures are born and die without us . . . and how many should?

Those girls ended up in a place similar to Wichita Canyon. I have to say that they were smart about where they went when things got bad. I come back, over and over, to the fact I should have done something sooner. The poet Rilke said something about after all, life is right, and I think everything happened exactly the way it was supposed to happen. But I would have rewritten this story.

Those girls are like daughters to me now. When people share hard times or work side by side, it is easy to build an intimacy that transcends the actual minutes or hours they've known each other. That's how it is with cowboy crews and, I suppose, all different kinds of crews of men who work and live together. When you've held up your end of a job, and demanded the same from every man around you, it just seems right to trust that man when the work day is over. When there is a big wreck, you figure out right away which man you want to be your compadre, and whether or not you welcome sharing space with him around the fire at night. I'd share everything I own with those two girls, though I figure it's a good thing they've gone on to their own lives.

It is flattering for an old man to have someone around who wants to hear his stories, wants to see what he sees, wants to know some of what he knows. We all want to pass something along, and I am no different. Charlie's always wanted to be a cowboy, and I could give her some of that. I could give her some of what I had learned over the years, and it was good for my ego because she soaked it up like a sponge. Whether we were gathering cows or packing mules or trailing something up, she made a good companion, a good student.

When I came here to Cottonwood, I went back to my lonesome ways, doing all I could alone until I needed the crew. The first few seasons I would call the new general manager and the cow boss would come over with the bunkhouse guys and we'd brand or wean or what-have-you, but then I got to where I would just borrow one or two of the quiet ones, or call Dave Cameron to come help me, get him out of the mine for a day or two. When Charlie started hanging around, I got her a paycheck for a few seasons and she was good help. Charlie paid attention and I didn't have to tell her things twice—though, of course, all old men repeat themselves.

I've never wanted to be perfect, just happy.

Katy took a break from reading to tote her camera around through all of the outbuildings and even a little ways down the creek. She found some empty containers perfect for packing up books and spent some time with old bindings and library smells in her hands before she went back to the handwritten letter. With only one legal pad to go, she was reluctant, almost, to continue . . . and yet, the story drew her, just as the warm sunshine of spring was drawing the green.

I always wished I had tried harder with Hope's kids, you know. I wish I had shown them how to have more fun. It seemed like there was always a job that needed doing and it didn't leave room for kids, or teaching them, or toting them along. When they got tired or hot or hungry, I got irritated, and it ruined our time together. Looking back, I can see, with an old man's clarity, that people are more important than the job that is always going to be pressing on a man. I wish I had known that then. Anna taught me to have fun, but I didn't carry those lessons forward much—not until it was too late.

Maybe not having children of my own, having been on the fringes of Hope's children's lives, maybe that was why I took to Charlie so much.

I messed up with my stepson. He was such a gawky young man, all elbows and knees and eager to please when I married Hope. I had an idea that he was going to be the one to receive my arrogant knowledge. I had to start from square one with that boy . . . or at least I should have. I should have started with How to Saddle a Horse 101, but I expected that a kid from a small rural town would know some things, or would figure things out on his own. I wish I had slowed down, taken care to meet him where he was, but the job could never wait. The job was too important. I dragged that poor boy all over hell and creation, and to be honest, I never once tried to help him see the wonder of it all. Before long, he got more interested in flying planes and dissecting motors than mucking around with a cow or a horse. And I don't blame him. He gave me a chance, but I never gave him one.

One Christmas here awhile back, he held his wine glass out towards me, and told the whole gathering that I am one of his heroes, that he is grateful for my hard ways. I've thought a lot about that evening, how everyone looked at me as if I am a relic from times past. I sure wish I had been less of a hero to that boy and more of a dad, that he felt less of a need to toast me on the holidays and more of a need to come hang out in my world.

It had only been raining for about five minutes, but all three of the riders were as wet as if they had jumped in the creek. The old man in the lead leaned his head back and looked straight up into the deluge and laughed out loud. "We'll take a rain or a calf any day, huh, girls!" The redheaded girl looked at him as if he were crazy. And he *was* a little crazy, crazy with relief and grief and love and hurt and an intense sense of the ludicrous as the trio neared the small barn beside the small house under huge cottonwood trees that were ancient as far as cottonwood trees ever get ancient. The other girl grinned and caught the old man's mood, laughing with delight at the way the day had turned from blistering hot to humid and rumbling to so wet that she thought a fish might bump her on the nose at any moment.

The three dismounted, and neither girl saw Uncle Bill wince and hold his arm closer to his side. Charlie began to help him unsaddle the horses and unlash the loads on the mules as quickly as wet knots and leather allowed, taking care of the stock and the tack as if the rain wasn't making it hard to breathe, much less move in the deepening mud.

Julia stood back in the relative dry of the saddle house, shivering and dripping, feeling helpless and in the way. "You two are crazy."

Charlie and Bill laughed. "Great tracking tomorrow, huh, Uncle Bill?"

Bill grinned at the girl. "I ain't lost nothing lately that I haven't already found. Maybe we'll take the day off! Rain on the ground is like shaking an Etch-A-Sketch. Like shaking an Etch-A-Sketch!"

The young women ran towards the camp house, blonde and red hair streaming as the thunder rumbled one last time and the late summer monsoon marched along at a more sedate pace. The old man came behind the girls, tired and hungry and heartsore.

A clean slate, he thought, if there is such a thing as a clean slate . . . .

Julia's story . . . cont.

It was hard to be at Cottonwood after being in Slide Canyon. For one thing, I had been honest with Charlie about the future and she wasn't taking it well. For another, Mark started driving out every night as if he were courting me, and I owed it to us both to let him. The sheriff came out, too, but after talking to the three of us, he went back to town, and we didn't hear from him again. I guess Cody Jack wasn't enough of a missing person to cause much uproar, or maybe he wasn't enough of a person, missing or otherwise. I said so to Uncle Bill and he looked sad. He said everyone ought to have someone who loves him enough to look for him when he goes missing.

Mandy and Rick drove out to check on me. Rick stood on the porch with Uncle Bill and, as they conversed, his face kept registering surprise. I wish I could have eavesdropped. Mandy fussed over me for a little while, but Mandy never fusses long. She'd rather talk about moon phases and seasons and archetypes and her latest craze. They didn't stay but one afternoon, and then it was just the three of us again. The only thing Rick said to me, before they left, was that I always, always had a home with them, but that sometimes the easiest way out of a tough spot is through. And of course, he's Rick, which means he's right.

I don't remember what all we did during those weeks. I know we played cards and listened to Uncle Bill play the fiddle or tell cowboy stories, some of them more than once. Charlie cooked or hiked for hours down the creek or sat in the porch

swing or went off on a horse to do some chore for Uncle Bill.
I tended those silly vegetables we had planted like a whole
lifetime before. And I read books from Uncle Bill's shelves,
discovered Henry Herbert Knibbs. For some reason, I began
to think of my thesis again. I slept and made some plans. I
had thought at the beginning that I would be going back to
Mandy and Rick's for awhile, and I wanted Charlie to make
some plans, too. I wanted Charlie to start living a real life,
go to school, grow some ambition. We argued about it every
day until one afternoon when Charlie was gone off down the
canyon again with that sturdy way of walking that makes me
ache inside.

Uncle Bill came up from the barn and sat on the porch with
me. He told me that it was okay for me to be making plans
but that we can't make plans for other people, that we can't
play God and arrange someone else's life according to how
we think they should live. He pointed out how terribly lonely
and miserable and out of place Charlie would be on a college
campus. He pointed out how Charlie's heart had been just a
little bit broken over the last few weeks. Mandy has always
said that the oldest religion in the world is Do No Harm.
Uncle Bill made me realize that no matter how carefully we
try to do no harm, we can't take one single step, not one single
breath, without affecting the world around us. For all of that,
though, I am still glad that Charlie and I had that summer, still
glad we loved each other, even if our love didn't match, didn't
come out the way Charlie imagined it would. It's like Uncle
Bill pointed out—we can never have too much love in our
lives. And then he added, "Or kindness."

That afternoon with Uncle Bill will stay with me forever.
I remember at one point I looked over at him, and he was

157

staring at some birds circling high over one of the peaks. I don't know why, but I asked him where he wanted to be buried someday. He looked at me hard and said not on Eagle Peak. Not on Eagle Peak.

I've got to get down to telling this story. I've filled up four legal pads talking about myself and the past just like the old man I didn't want to become.

Katy looked up from the page and laughed. "Uncle Bill, you are doing just fine." She pointed her finger at the urn. "I like your story. I sure do."

It was the hottest part of July when Charlie and Julia ran away, and I will always wonder what was going through Charlie's head. Why didn't she run toward the town, toward the pavement, toward all that is civilized? I don't understand what she did, but then again, I have never been a woman overpowered by a man, running in fear of more pain. It's been a long time since I've known real fear. After all, what does a man my age have to fear? Death? That would be silly. I can say for certain that I fear being a drooling burden on someone someday, living like ol' Dave Cameron, but I won't let that happen. When a job has to be done, there is no room for fear.

Richard Benson always said that every human being is doing the best he can in any given moment. Charlie sure did some smart things on the day she ran off. She took most of the things she needed to survive and to take care of Julia. I felt proud like a father when I realized she left Live Oak Camp in the middle of the saddle horses to cover her tracks. Not that Cody Jack could track himself to the outhouse and back, but when I think of all the gals in the world who can only think about their nails and their hair and their favorite movie star, I am proud of the way that girl headed out into the backcountry with two horses and a mule. I am proud of the way she took care of her friend.

My part started when Mark showed up here. He looked like he hadn't had much sleep and had drunk too much coffee, and I suppose both were true.

I've seen a couple of general managers come and go since I turned the position over, and I have to say that I like Mark. He's a good kid . . . a good man, I should say. Simple. Passionate in his own way, pretty religious here lately, but that is a disease that a lot of people get and sometimes recover from. I am more Buddhist than anything else, or maybe a throwback to the old ways of believing, the old ways of honoring nature, worshiping the creation more than a creator I have to imagine in my own mind. I've read the Bible just like I've read several books of wisdom. One of my favorite verses is the one about how each man must work out his own salvation in fear and trembling. I like that part. In fear and trembling. Everyone gets as much Jesus in his life as he needs, and some, like Mark, need a bigger dose. He's one of those people who embrace an idea like a bulldog and won't let go. Except he's more like a desert snapping turtle than a bulldog. Plodding, deliberate, able to pull into his own secret place when he needs to.

Katy stopped reading here because a sheet of paper was taped across the next few paragraphs, creating two layers. The top layer read:

February 20—
Dear Katy-girl,

If you've gotten this far, I tip my hat. You've got more grit than even I gave you credit for. However, the next bit is about you, and if I were to do the right thing, I would tear it out. But this morning I found my old dog, Copper, dead beside the stove when I got up to put the coffee on. I have been letting him sleep inside on cold nights for the past couple of years. I regret that I didn't scratch behind his ears one more time before I went to bed last night. I don't want to do the right thing with this story. I want to do the brave thing. So, I am leaving these paragraphs as they are. If they embarrass you, I am sorry. If they weren't true, I'd be the first to throw them out. But they are, and truth has to matter for something in a story.
Your biggest fan, Uncle Bill

Katy carefully lifted the taped on layer and resumed reading underneath.

I watched Mark fall in love one summer a few years ago. Not with Julia, but with Katy. Every male old enough to piss behind the barn fell in love with Katy that summer. None of us could help it. She is, in many ways, every man's dream. She comes across as icy and contained, but truly, down deep, she is wild and flamboyant, one of those gals who would pose nude and never think a thing about it other than to hope her best side was to the camera. I saw a poster once, one of those tourism posters advertising some river trip, showing the face of a canyon wall with a woman under a waterfall, hair hanging down her back, just the curve of her buttocks showing, the suggestion of a curve of one breast, softness surrounded by rock, outward water suggestive of inward succulence, bare feet on a slick slab. When I think of Katy, I think of that poster.

Katy's tough, too. She came out to the ranch to work and though she is one of the actual heirs to this land, she really worked. Not like some of her relatives who have come out and played at working. Katy made a hand. She did all that was expected of her and more. And she captured our hearts. She isn't sweet, but she is smart, and funny, and strong, and generous. She entered into ranch life, didn't blend in exactly, but made her own spot amongst us. I will always be grateful that after we got to know each other, Katy showed me her softer side. She always had her camera close at hand and took some startling portraits of the people on the ranch. I think everyone values the gifts she made of them, though I don't think everyone understands them.

Mark took an awful fall. He was interning under the last general manager, being groomed for the job between college semesters. I heard that Katy broke up with him by Thanksgiving, but they had one of those grand summer flings that are hard to get over. And I think he fell much harder than she did. After all, a man like Mark could spend his lifetime trying to make a woman like Katy happy, not realizing that the more he tries, the less she needs him.

After Katy finished college, she sent me postcards from all over the world. I wonder if Mark saw them as they came through the office at headquarters where I pick up my mail. Did he see that she was in Brazil? Hungary? Australia? Tanzania? On the steppes with the shaggy ponies? Petting a whale, balanced in a tiny boat? The postcards were her own photographs, and in them I saw reflections of that tough leggy girl who gathered all of that long hair back into a careless ponytail and, just as carelessly, stole Mark's heart, stole all of our hearts.

Katy hadn't cried at Uncle Bill's funeral. Katy hadn't cried in the lawyer's office. She hadn't cried when Mark had called her to say that he had found Bill in bed late one afternoon, no longer breathing. But sitting there on the couch where she would sleep for many nights, Katy rested her forehead on her knees and cried. Cried for Uncle Bill. Cried for Julia. Cried for Charlie. Cried for Mark. Cried for that old Jasper horse. Cried for Copper. Cried for Budroe and Jeb having lost their main man. Cried because it was time and crying was exactly the right thing to do.

Mark was plenty upset when he got here. Said Julia had left him and he'd found her at Live Oak but that they had agreed that she'd stay there with Charlie for a few days. Said he went back out to Live Oak three days later and found no trace of Julia or Charlie, and Julia's car was still at headquarters.

Mark couldn't say for certain that the girls hadn't left in Charlie's little truck and gone off somewhere for a little fun. All he knew for sure was that the girls were missing and so was Cody Jack. He had the presence of mind to check the saddle house and see that the pack gear was gone, too, so he had an idea that they had gone into the backcountry. The slashed tires on Cody Jack's ranch truck had Mark plenty worried, but I also witnessed a heavy pride in Mark that made him come to me instead of calling the law. After all, his position on the ranch wouldn't have stood much scandal. His wife had left him and was now missing along with another woman. Mark looked plenty scared, plenty sick, plenty worried.

I hoped, and believed then, that Cody Jack had left the country for good. I also figured, rightly, that Charlie didn't want to be found right away, by anyone. Mark argued with me for waiting until morning, but those girls had already been gone for three days. One more night wasn't going to change anything, and in a way, I felt like it was my gift to them. If I had known how close I came to being wrong, I wouldn't have slept that night. I would have trailed up those girls by moonlight.

The next morning I made up a pack with some medical supplies, some food, a bottle of whiskey, and made a show of driving over to Live Oak to start my search. I convinced Mark to make himself useful and go with one of the other guys to retrieve my truck, bring it back to Benson headquarters. The girls' tracks weren't hard to pick up after I left that dadburned horse pasture, bless Charlie's conniving little heart, but then, I had a good idea which way they were headed and cut for tracks in that direction first. It wasn't long until Budroe, Jeb, and I were in a little jig trot headed for Slide Canyon.

Katy clambered up the last steep lip to the top of the ridge. She held a slip of paper in one hand, her phone in the other. The phone never, ever made her feel smart. The ring in her ear was jarring; after all, she'd listened to nothing electronic except the whirring of the refrigerator for many days.

"Anna Delgado's office. How may I help you?"

All of a sudden, the poems made sense.

When Katy swiped the screen to end the call a few minutes later, she stood and looked over the landscape while fragments of poetry sang themselves in her head.

I hope you turn the TV off, bathe in woodsmoke,
play cribbage on an endless winter night,
I hope for you surprising springs in deep canyons,
and love, and a golden eagle above the cliffs in flight.

●

Songbirds weave in and out of the bushes
And I become one of them
As I weave
With words and with wire.

●

Sorting in bright baked pens,
Gooseneck gates rattle loudly in the heat.
We've memorized that blank sky—
notice the moment that cottonball cloud puffs—
like a changed word in our familiar song.
We look away.

Before she climbed back down the slope, Katy called Mark to fill him in on the plan.

Later that evening, Julia raised startled eyes from her meal. "Anna Delgado? THE Anna Delgado? She's coming here?"

"Evidently. That's what Katy said. Katy said you'd fill me in on who she …" Mark watched his wife move swiftly away from the table and to the bookshelves in a whirl that denied how round she had gotten with child.

"I can't believe you don't know who she is! Anna Delgado!" Julia pulled five slim volumes from the shelf and brought them to thump gently in front of her amused but unabashedly clueless husband. "Only the most wonderful, my favorite, award-winning poet! Anna Delgado!"

Mark looked at the beautiful pile of books in front of him, but they were nothing to him compared to the beauty that was his wife.

It is morning, still so early that the stars and birds have not yet realized it. Only people who cannot sleep stand looking at their own reflections in dark windows while the scent of coffee truly says morning.

Cottonwood Camp is nestled in Cottonwood Creek on the Cottonwood side of the ranch, and the old man who moved here when he was just beginning to be an old man pours his first cup into a hand-thrown pottery mug. He sets the percolator down gently on the clay trivet, always aware of his guests asleep in his bedroom. A rolled-up canvas bedroll propped in the corner testifies to where he spent the night.

His mind should have been on those guests soundly sleeping the sleep of the young, but instead he is thinking of Eagle Peak, of things that happened, of things that are done and can never be undone. He is thinking of the conversation the night before when he told Charlie not to worry, not to worry about Cody Jack ever again. Ever. And while he said the words, he looked up at the peak rising above Cottonwood Canyon, looked up at the buzzards making their evening circles above the rock.

Charlie's story . . . cont.

You are going to think I'm crazy. Hell, maybe I am a little
crazy. But remember the day of Uncle Bill's funeral? Well,
when it was all done, I needed to get away, get away from all
that had happened, away from all that had not gone the way
I had thought it would, away from the looks the bunkhouse
guys give me full of the gossip they've heard. Away from
Julia's round belly and Mark's hand under her elbow as if she
is fragile. I came here, came right here to this camp. I lay on
this front porch and did my crying for Uncle Bill here. Cried
the whole afternoon away, cried for how I loved Julia, cried
for her going back to Mark, cried for Uncle Bill, cried for
myself if the truth be known—and then I scared myself. As
I lay here, not crying much anymore, just breathing hard and
sniffling, I heard a fiddle, Uncle Bill's fiddle, just a'playin' and
a'playin', all of those sweet, sweet songs that I'd heard him
play a hundred times.

Even with my heart pounding and my head telling me I was
crazy, my ears could still hear that fiddle music, not coming
from one place in particular, just echoing up and down the
creek. Right in that moment, I knew I missed Uncle Bill more
than I missed my own daddy. Right in that moment I knew
that he had loved me, really truly loved me, maybe like no one
else ever has before or ever will again. Right in that moment, I
knew that I had loved him too and wished with all of my heart
that I could have him back, even wished he had not been
fifty-something years older than me. Right in that moment I

remembered what he said, "And you, Charlie, are like earth and wind and fire, with a little rain thrown in to smell good." Right in that moment, I knew that I was going to be okay.

Julia loves me, you know, even if it isn't the same as I love her.

I guess you are all grown up when you realize that it is okay to love in different ways. You know you are all grown up when you realize that it is okay to love *more*. You know you are all grown up when you realize that, even with your heart feeling like it has the mother of all hangovers, you are going to love again.

There are worse things than being alone. If Uncle Bill didn't teach me anything, he taught me that.

An elegant woman with white hair and very blue eyes stepped from the car at headquarters and stood looking around her as if she were in a museum. She smiled, but barely, when she shook Katy's hand.

"If they made a movie, this would be the set of my lost years." She sighed as if to shake away the past and pulled a neat suitcase from the back seat. When Katy explained to Anna that she was welcome to stay in the Big House at headquarters, the older woman shook her head emphatically.

"No. I want go to Bill's camp. Cottonwood, right? No, my dear, if you don't mind, I want to go there." Anna loaded her case in the truck and the Anna whom Katy had originally pictured began to come back into focus.

The words "famous poet" faded into a backdrop of ignorable unimportance as the evening aged. Anna came from Bill's bedroom wearing jeans and a striped work shirt with the sleeves rolled up above her elbows. She tapped the stack of yellow legal pads on the table and said with some humor, "I see I must take a day, no? Trust Billy Morgan to leave a job for me to do! Two jobs…."

The urn seemed to glow brighter in her presence.

The next day, Anna read Bill's words in privacy while Katy tapped furiously on her laptop at the table. She wrote a plea to the Board of Directors, explaining her plan to stay on the ranch to learn everything she could about the management and the men and the land, as well as to pursue her own dream of words and images that bolstered each other, that told a story, that told more than one story.

Anna came into the house in the late evening and placed the stack of tablets on the table and then gave them a little shove with her hands, pushed them away.

"Ha. Hard to believe he's gone." She walked over and poured three fingers of whiskey.

"Hit save on that thing. I've got questions."

Katy grinned at the older woman's bossy tone and fixed her own drink, pulling a tray of vegetables and dips and snacks out of the refrigerator.

"So, where are those girls now?"

Katy bit into a slice of pita bread spread with hummus and chewed . . . still smiling.

"Well, let's see. I boxed up books and pieces of this and that for days, delivered them all over the place. Julia is at headquarters, happily back with Mark, looking like an obscene pixie with an enormous belly. It is a bit disconcerting."

Anna laughed, and when Anna laughed, Katy wished, for the first and last time in her life, that she was a man, a man strong and wise and handsome, worthy to place his forehead against the high and beautiful one of the poet across from her. Her throat filled with longing to be in love with and be loved by someone like Anna. And for the first time ever, she thought the young William Morgan had been a fool.

"Oh, whew! I am so glad to be alive!" The older woman wiped her eyes on her sleeve and took a sip of whiskey. "Life is a kick, now isn't it?"

Katy swallowed in surprise. Why, of course. That is what grief seemed to be teaching her. To laugh. To be grateful she was alive. She looked at Anna and the blue eyes above the whiskey glass sparkled with understanding. Katy swallowed again and went on, "Julia is also going to be royally pissed that she doesn't get to meet you. She is, evidently, a big fan."

Anna sat still. "Maybe next time. This time is for Bill."

The two women made the slightest toast toward each other and toward the urn.

Katy continued. "And Charlie is back on the 3R, back in the little trailer behind the cook house, breaking their horses, but you know, I think she has other plans. When I took her boxes of books by, she said that she is going to the Sierras to pack mules for a season. Seems the 3R is willing to have her back for the winter . . . she can split her time. And maybe this isn't mine to tell, but she is the heir to Bill's little nest egg, the one my uncle left him so long ago. It feels right, doesn't it?"

Anna nodded. "I'd like to meet her, if you don't mind. Perhaps when we drive to the south side tomorrow. I think Charlie is the one I need to meet."

Spring now lay soft across the land, and the mating frogs chorused through the night.

Mark and Katy stood side by side and watched Anna drive away toward the highway. It had been a long day that started very early with Mark saddling up a horse and hooking the trailer up to Katy's ranch truck. Katy had driven Anna and Bill's ashes over to South Camp on the 3R. The little woman had hopped up on the horse as if she were two decades younger and ridden away with a plastic zip-top bag.

The night before the two women had transferred Uncle Bill into the baggie when Anna decided carrying an urn would be impractical.

Katy sat on the wheel well of the trailer to wait for her return and thought of the conversation that had cleaved the night before until it was almost morning. Anna had told her about Bill as a younger man, had spoken of the 3R and their time there, and had spoken to Katy of her Uncle Richard. She held the olla in her hands and told Katy that she was glad it now belonged to her. She packed the fiddle away carefully, her unpinned white hair hiding the tears that fell into the case along with it. She, too, had stood at dusk looking down Cottonwood Creek for a long time, as if listening for Bill there.

On the drive to the canyon with Bill's ashes, Anna had pointed out a long mesa in the distance.

"Let me tell you a funny story and then this old woman won't bore you anymore. When Bill was getting ready to turn the 3R over, we had to rebuild a stretch of fence up there on that mesa. We had an old beater Jeep to use as a fencing rig so we loaded our camp and off we went. Such an adventure, but really only work. Everything is an adventure when you are young and in love …"

Her voice didn't break so much as fade for a bit then come back just as strong.

"We moved along that stretch of fence with new wire and stretchers and saws and stays, and I started noticing what I *thought* were wild onions. I had this grand idea that I would dig them and add them to our dinner. I spent one whole day being less help than I could have because I found this great digging stick. I moved from one plant to another, one tiny blue flower on a long rising stem to another, digging up the starchy root. Only thing is, that evening, as I was browning meat over the fire and adding in cans of stuff to make burritos, I wondered why these "wild onions," and I had a *pile* of them, didn't *smell* like onions. I figured, well, maybe wild onions were just much milder than normal ones. We ate those burritos, but those hard-won starchy little bulbs I had so carefully cleaned and sliced into the pan didn't *taste* like onions either! When we got back to the house two days later, I got out my plant book and found that I had not fed poor Bill wild onions, but another edible root plant called *blue dick!* I fed us both blue dick!"

Katy would never forget the beautiful woman's laughter, nor the soft sweet way she was with Charlie, though Katy stood back so she couldn't hear all that was said between them.

Now, Mark and Katy watched Anna Delgado's taillights leave the Benson Ranch.

"She seems young."

"Yeah, very."

"She doesn't seem famous."

"I don't think she is, in her mind."

"Did you get your interview?"

"No. She said I had Bill's story—that I didn't need hers." Katy didn't mention that in exchange for the framed portrait of Bill with his fiddle tucked under his chin, Katy had been given the opportunity to photograph Anna as the sun sank in the sky, and that right before bedtime when Anna put her hand on her arm, Katy felt the old wound of her mother's death begin to heal. That was all too much to put out into the air right now.

Plus, in the dark of Uncle Bill's camp, Katy had decided that some of the story that had become a part of her needed to stay on the yellow pages and in her own memory. There was no need to cause any harm. Anna's presence had reinforced that decision.

As she turned to walk to her truck, Mark had made a little joke, Mark-style. "God's doing fine. Thanks for asking, Katy."

It made her grin all the way home.

In a lonely little trailer behind a cook shack on a ranch where a band of mares gives birth every spring to fifteen colts, give or take, life or death, a bouquet of wild flowers rises and droops from a glass jar that rests on the table. The jar once contained artichoke hearts.

I killed that boy, you know. I shot him and toted his sorry carcass up onto Eagle Peak. I killed him the moment I realized that no matter how smart I was, no matter how logical I was, no matter how right I was, nothing was going to stop him from hurting those girls. There was no way I could protect them. There was no way I was going to save him and myself and those girls. No way to save us all.

Truth is, I almost didn't get the job done. That boy was fast with his knife. But I healed . . . and there are worse wounds than a knife cut—wounds that never fully heal.

I let Anna down, way back when. I let Charlie down. All I could see when I looked in that boy's eyes was a fried brain. When he talked all big and doped up, every story I had heard about his cruelty and his temper echoed in my ears. I knew, after all that had happened, he had nothing to lose.

And I did. I did have something to lose. Still do. I have a lot to lose because I love breathing in and out. I love seeing the sunrise. But all of that is just blah, blah, blah. Just talk. It doesn't matter if I acted in self-defense or if it was a crime of passion or if it sprang from something mean and vengeful way down in my heart that came alive when I saw those quirt marks on Charlie's back. I killed that man, and he needed killing. I gave him a sky burial which is more decent than the conventional ways we dispose of people nowadays.

I wanted to tell a story of love, of rescue, of happy endings, but we don't always get to tell the story we'd choose. We can't mark out the hard parts.

Here is where I am supposed to say I'm sorry. It is human nature to apologize. How often do we hesitate to be ourselves, truly act as an individual without prefacing it with "I'm sorry?" Are we truly sorry or do we just think it is the right thing to say? I may be a little dramatic here at the end of my pages. I may be a little over the top here at the end of my life. Should I apologize? Or should I take my pen in hand and bear down a little harder so that there is an imprint of my words on the next page and the next and the next . . . write something good for those my heart holds dear.

What would I write?

Sing a little louder. Take fewer baths. Eat the spiciest, tastiest, meatiest parts. Read something that is pure mind candy, and then read something hard and weighty that changes the way you think. Lick the bowl clean. Be aware of the phases of the moon and the paths of the stars in the sky. Dance. Plant impractical seeds. Hug a horse, a dog, a storm, a stranger. Take a nap under a tree close to running water. Say I love you. Produce something of value. Create something of beauty. Stay up all night. Take off your clothes out of doors and let the cold water take your breath away. Sit on a rock naked while the hot sun acts as a towel. Laugh. Sing some more. Dream and write your dreams down just because. Say what you mean. And don't preface every single gift you give out into the world with I'm sorry.

And remember, love is a funny thing. Actually, it is <u>the</u> thing. It doesn't have to make sense. And it isn't something that you figure out how to do and then know how to do for the rest of your life.

Katy looked up. There were no more words on the yellow pages.

That night, as Katy stood on the porch, Wild Turkey 101 in hand, watching a few bats making swooping dives through the trees, she heard fiddle music echoing off down the canyon.

She raised her glass towards another legendary sunset on Cottonwood Creek.

Epilogue

Eagle Peak is nothing special. Just the apex of a boulder pile whose slopes are an armpit of cholla, agave, catclaw, and prickly pear. It takes a long time to climb to the top and a long time to pick a path back down. There is no easy way. There is nothing up there to see, just a pile of bones, and even those are scattered. A sky burial is best for all whose hearts long to someday fly, to soar to the tops of places we want to see but don't always work up the energy to go on foot. A sky burial is also the way to go when there is nothing to be gained from everyone knowing you are dead and how you died. The only things that will puzzle the intrepid hiker someday are the remains of a saddle and bridle, a pair of boots, and a felt hat shoved way back in a crevice between two massive rocks, bigger than houses. But maybe a bobcat has already nested in them, or a pack rat has carried off the leather pieces for his own project, or maybe they'll rot away with rainfall and time.

It isn't important.

After all, the story is the thing.

Julia's Piña Colada Cake

1 yellow cake mix
1 can cream of coconut
1 can sweetened condensed milk
1 carton whipped topping

Prepare sheet cake according to directions. While it is baking, combine cream of coconut and sweetened condensed milk with a wire whisk.

When cake comes out of the oven, while it is still hot, poke holes in it at intervals with the handle of a wooden spoon. Pour coconut mixture over hot cake. Chill. Frost with whipped topping.

Uncle Bill's Beef Jerky

Slice flank steak or any steak or roast very thin with a sharp knife. Salt and pepper. Hang high until dried. Packs well.

Charlie's Cherry Pie

2 cans sour pie cherries, drain one can, retain juice of other
1 cup sugar mixed with 2 tablespoons flour
1 cup fruit juice (citrus is best)

Bring cherries and juice to a boil. Mash cherries with potato masher. Add other ingredients, stir well. Simmer until thickened. Add lump of butter the size of a hen's egg.

Pour into unbaked pie shell, top with whole or lattice crust. Bake at 375° for one hour.

Acknowledgements

I have been listening to cowboy stories since before I was born. I owe my life as a writer to those stories and to those storytellers: Robert Raymond Hale, Tom Hale, Ray Fitzgerald, Nick Auker, George Deering, Ricky Bud Clark, Kidd Ybarra, Ross Knox, Gail Steiger, Harry Chiantaretto, Matt Bates, men named Garlick and Henderson, men from Texas and South Dakota and Arizona and Nevada and Oklahoma. Wherever livestock men gather, stories are told. And retold.

I am grateful to Duke and Kimberly for taking a chance on something this unconventionally structured. I am grateful to Steve Atkinson for his beautiful artwork and design and for his and Ann's friendship. Steve, in my estimation, you *are* the Grand Poobah.

I am grateful to Lily Rose Auker who reads every manuscript multiple times and to Matt Bates who told me there had to be a fight. He was right.

Once upon a time, Peggy Krantz, my cousin who is also my sister, wrote some words to me about living life that were so beautiful I gave them to Uncle Bill to say. Thanks, Peg. I owe you.

My thanks to all the cowmen who will take a rain or a calf any day.

RIP, Jake. September 2014

About Amy Hale Auker

Amy Hale Auker writes and thrives on a ranch in Arizona where she is having a love affair with rocks, mountains, piñon and juniper forests, the weather, and her songwriter husband who is also foreman of the ranch.

Author of WILLA Award winning *Rightful Place* (2011) and *Winter of Beauty* (2013), she guides her readers to a place where the bats fly, lizards do pushups on the rocks, bears leave barefoot prints in the dirt. Where hummingbirds do rain dances in August, spiders weave for their food, and poetry is in the chrysalis and the cocoon. She tells stories about the real world where things grow up out of the ground, where the miracle of life happens over and over again, where people can and do survive without malls or Arby's. Amy believes that what you put out there is what you get back, and that if you do the good, hard work you will be rewarded. Come, visit the world she lives in.

www.amyhaleauker.com